"You couldn't trust me completely then, and I cannot trust you now. And that is why you will never be my wife."

Well, she'd asked for it, Grace told herself unhappily.

"So that's it," she said drearily. "That's all there is to say."

"Not entirely." Constantine surprised her by coming back swiftly. "The question is, where do we go from here?"

"Go? Is there anywhere to go?"

"Of course." He sounded stunned that she should have doubted it.

"But—but you don't love me. You don't trust me. So what basis do we have for any sort of relationship?"

"The perfect basis for the kind of relationship I have in mind."

GREEK TYCOONS

Men who have everything—except a bride

Wealth, power, charm—what else could a heart-stoppingly handsome tycoon need? Meet Constantine, Dio, Andreas and Nikolas, four gorgeous Greek billionaires who are each in need of a wife. Over the next few months, look out for the stories in which each one of these tycoons meets his match and decides that he *has* to have her...*whatever* it takes!

Look out for:

January 2000:
Constantine's Revenge by Kate Walker
March 2000:
Expectant Bride by Lynne Graham
May 2000:
The Tycoon's Bride by Michelle Reid
June 2000:
The Millionaire's Virgin by Anne Mather

KATE WALKER

Constantine's Revenge

GREEK TYCOONS

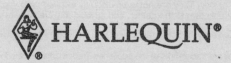

HARLEQUIN®

TORONTO • NEW YORK • LONDON
AMSTERDAM • PARIS • SYDNEY • HAMBURG
STOCKHOLM • ATHENS • TOKYO • MILAN • MADRID
PRAGUE • WARSAW • BUDAPEST • AUCKLAND

ISBN 0-373-12082-6

CONSTANTINE'S REVENGE

First North American Publication 2000.

Copyright © 1999 by Kate Walker.

Visit us at www.romance.net

Printed in U.S.A.

CHAPTER ONE

It HAD begun with a knock at the door.

Such a simple thing and yet it had changed Grace's life for ever. It had taken her happiness, her dreams of a future, and ripped them into tiny shreds. And as a result, even now, two years later, she still had to nerve herself to answer any summons from someone on the outside of the house.

'Gracie, sweetie!' Ivan's voice reached her from the kitchen, where he was busy creating his own devilishly intoxicating version of a fruit punch. 'Are you going to answer that or just stand and stare at the door all day?'

'Of course I am!'

She hadn't even been aware that that was what she had been doing, Grace realised as, with a fierce little mental shake, she pushed herself into action. It was stupid to react in this way. After all, it was fully twenty-four months since that appalling day. This wasn't her father's house, the place she had used to call home, but the elegant Victorian building where Ivan had the ground-floor flat. And nothing could be more different from the careful preparations for the elaborate society wedding of the past than the casual, noisily crowded atmosphere of the party her friend was giving to celebrate his thirtieth birthday.

'I didn't know we were expecting anyone else!' she tossed over her shoulder, using laughter to disguise the irrational uncertainty that still clutched at her stomach as she hurried to answer a second imperious knock at the door. 'Just how many people have you invited? The place is bursting at the seams already.'

'A party isn't a party until you don't have room to breathe!'

Grace barely heard Ivan's response. Joking hadn't helped. If anything, the crazy feeling of apprehension had grown worse. She felt like some nervous cat, scenting the approach of an aggressive intruder into its territory, every fine blonde hair lifting at the back of her neck, her soft grey eyes clouded and shadowy.

Lightning couldn't strike twice! she told herself. At least not the sort of lightning she had in mind.

White teeth digging sharply into the softness of her lower lip, she dragged in a deep, fortifying breath before grasping the handle firmly and pulling at the door.

It came open far more swiftly than she had anticipated, flying back towards her with a force that almost knocked her off balance, so that she staggered slightly, struggling to keep upright.

'Steady...'

A deep, drawling voice, rich as honeyed cream, was the first thing she registered. Then two other facts hit home at the same time, with the force of a devastating blow in the pit of her stomach.

Two frighteningly significant facts. Two disturbingly familiar and shockingly vividly remembered details about the man before her that made her thoughts reel, her head spinning sickeningly.

Deep, dark eyes. Eyes black as jet, and every bit as hard. Their stunning colour and blazing intensity had been etched into her memory long ago, impossible to erase. And that sensual voice, exotically accented, seemed to coil around her nerves, tightening and twisting them until they screamed.

Other images bombarded her. Smooth olive-toned skin, a strong jaw, a beautiful mouth with a surprisingly full lower lip. Hair black as a raven's wing, cropped uncompromisingly short in order to subdue a rebellious tendency to curl. Suddenly it was as if some cruel hand had reached out from the past, snatching hold of her and dragging her back into the tumult of emotions she had experienced then.

'Are you all right?'

Strong hands had fastened over her arms, supporting her, and only when she was secure on her feet did the tall, dark man actually look into her face.

'*You!*' he said sharply, his expression changing instantly from one of concern to a look of pure contempt that seared over Grace's already rawly sensitive skin. 'I didn't recognise you, looking like that.'

Every vital function in her body seemed to have shut down in shock. She had to tell herself to breathe, her heart to beat. Lightning *could* strike twice, it seemed. Certainly Greek lightning could. Because the force of the most violent electrical storm had always been the effect that this man had had on her.

'Constantine!'

Her tongue felt clumsy as it tangled around the name that she had refused to speak for so long. The name she had promised herself she would never, ever use again if she could help it. But now sheer shock and a sense of unbelieving horror had forced it from her against her will.

'What are you doing here?'

The look he turned on her burned with cynical disbelief. Only an idiot would have had the stupidity to ask that question, his lofty disdain declared. And if there was one thing that Constantine Kiriazis was quite unprepared to tolerate then it was the presence of any sort of a fool.

'I was invited,' he declared, his voice as curt as his movements as he belatedly became aware of the way that he was still holding her, long, tanned hands on her arms, the immaculately manicured fingers incongruous against the shabby, well-worn leather of her jacket.

With a fastidious gesture that communicated only too clearly the feeling that simply to touch her had somehow contaminated him, he abruptly let her go and stepped away from her side. The move spoke eloquently of a mental distance that was far, far greater than the few centimetres that actually separated them.

'This *is* where the party's being held?'

With a brusque nod of her head Grace dismissed the unnecessary question. The sheer volume of noise behind her, the music and laughter, the loud buzz of fifty or more different conversations made a nonsense of the fact that he had even asked it.

'But Ivan wouldn't have invited you!'

The cynical lift of one black, straight brow mocked at her vehemence, shaking the certainty of her conviction without a single word.

'Tell me, my sweet Grace, do you really believe that I would appear here, dressed like this...?' An arrogant sweep of his hand swept down the powerful length of his body, drawing her clouded grey eyes unwillingly after it. 'Without the excuse of your crazy friend's theme party to justify it?'

Silently Grace cursed herself for being every sort of a fool. She hadn't wanted even to *look* at him. But with that single haughty gesture he had forced her to do just that. And, having looked, she found herself incapable of turning away again.

She didn't want to be reminded of the lean power and strength of Constantine's body. Didn't want to recall the honed muscle and hard bone that she had once known so intimately. It hurt just to remember how it had felt to be held in those arms, to be crushed close to the wall of that chest, feel that sensual mouth on her own.

'I don't think you've exactly understood the theme of tonight.'

Furious control gave her words a biting coldness, and her clear grey eyes were like shards of silvery ice as she let her gaze run back up the length of his tall frame in an expression of disdain that matched his own of only moments earlier. Matched and outstripped it as she let her full mouth curl derisively.

'The idea is that this is a Turn Back the Clock party. Ivan's painfully aware of the fact that at midnight he'll be thirty, that he'll have left his twenties behind for ever. Everyone is to dress in the sort of clothes they would have worn ten years ago, so that just for tonight he can pretend...'

'Do you think I don't know that?' Constantine snapped, his accent deepening as anger marked his voice. 'I do not need you to explain what I already understand perfectly. And if I had any doubts then the distressingly unflattering outfit you are wearing would erase them once and for all.'

'At least I entered into the spirit of things!' Grace flashed back at him, her chin lifting in angry defiance.

She didn't need to be reminded that what she was wearing was so very different from the way he was used to seeing her. The way anyone was used to seeing her. Ten years ago she had been a mere fourteen, and then the skintight denim jeans worn with a white sleeveless tee shirt and a leather biker jacket over the top had been her ideal of relaxed weekend clothing.

Dressing to come to the party tonight, she had actually thought her chosen costume was quite fun. That the uncharacteristic way she had done her hair, tousling the blonde sleekness into wild disarray, together with the use of much more make-up than usual, particularly around her wide grey eyes, made her look younger and more relaxed. She had smiled to see herself looking totally unlike the elegant, controlled Grace Vernon her workmates at the advertising agency would have recognised.

But now, faced with Constantine's obvious censure, she felt the bubble of euphoria that had buoyed her up burst painfully sharply, leaving her limp and miserably deflated. What had seemed light-hearted and fun now seemed gauche and unsophisticated in the extreme, making her shift uncomfortably from one foot to another as once more Constantine's jet-black gaze seared over her in a way that brought a burning rush of colour to her pale cheeks. How she longed for the protection of her usual refined way of dressing.

If she had known he would be here tonight she would have worn something that oozed sophistication and would have knocked him dead. Something that would have shown him just what he was missing. What he had discarded so brutally when he had tossed her aside, declaring that she wasn't fit to be his wife.

If she had known he would be here...!

Who was she kidding? If she had even so much as suspected that Constantine Kiriazis was in England, let alone in the capital, where she and Ivan lived, she would have turned and run, putting as much distance as was possible between herself and the man she had once loved so desperately.

'I bothered to dress up, while you...'

'And what, precisely, is wrong with what I'm wearing?' Constantine enquired with a silky menace that sent a sneaking shiver down her spine.

'It's hardly *fun*, is it? I mean, it's so...'

Words failed her. The only ones that sprang to mind were

such that she clamped her mouth tight shut on them, refusing to let them out.

The truth was that his outfit was pure *Constantine*, somehow displaying outwardly the very essence of the man.

The long black cashmere overcoat he wore against the
unexpectedly bitter winds of the last evening in March had
to have been handmade and superbly tailored into its perfect fit on his athletic form. It spoke of wealth, more wealth
than the average person could even begin to dream of, but
an affluence that was very definitely old money. Riches that
had been in the family for so long that they no longer even
registered on their owner's mind. And they certainly needed
no show or ostentation to draw attention to their existence.

Constantine Kiriazis had never flaunted the trappings of
the fortune she knew he possessed, both from having grown
up as the son of a very rich man and from having earned
a second, equally huge amount in his own right. His
clothes, like the rest of the man, were always exquisite but
severely restrained, the heavy, square-faced gold watch he
wore on his wrist the only ornament he ever indulged in.

Underneath the luxurious overcoat he wore equally stark
black and white: a pristine shirt, bow tie, close-fitting black
trousers and, unexpectedly, a tailored waistcoat, but no
jacket. In contrast to the weird and colourful assortment of
clothing worn by the other guests in response to Ivan's
choice of the theme for his party, he looked polished, sophisticated, totally disciplined, not at all in the mood for a
party.

'So...?' Constantine echoed, a dangerous edge to his
voice.

'So—controlled, so...'

She was only too well aware of the way that her own
complicated feelings were setting her nerves on edge, making her take exception over what was in fact very far from

her real preoccupation. She wanted—needed—to drag her thoughts away from their wanton fixation on the very masculine body beneath the fine clothes, the devastatingly sexual male animal that she knew Constantine to be.

'You look like nothing so much as a waiter.'

Something violent flared in the depths of those stunning eyes at her tone, and she actually heard his strong white teeth snap together, as if he had bitten back the furious outburst he had been about to make. She knew her remark had caught him on the raw, stinging the fierce pride that was so much a part of his character.

'It runs in the genes,' he had told her once. 'The ancient Greeks were cursed with it—the *hubris* that so often brought about their downfall. These days we call it *perifania*, but the feeling is exactly the same.'

'It might interest you to know, my sweet Grace,' he said now, 'that that is exactly how I am supposed to look.'

His tone was surprisingly soft, but laced through with a thread of darkness that revealed only too clearly the ruthlessness with which he had reined in his volatile temper.

'Ten years ago, when I was twenty-one and fresh out of university, my grandfather insisted that I learn about every aspect of his business empire—from the bottom up. I spent my first six months working as a waiter in one of the hotels owned by the Kiriazis Corporation.'

'Oh...'

It was all she could manage. Her lips were suddenly painfully dry and she moistened them nervously with her tongue. The movement froze as she saw those intent black eyes drop to fix on the small action that betrayed the chaotic state of her thoughts, and at the same moment the significance of what he had said came home to her on a rush of shock.

'Then—then Ivan *did* invite you?'

'Ivan invited me,' he acceded, moving at last into the small hallway and kicking the door shut behind him. The thud it made slamming home into its frame had such a sound of finality that Grace shuddered on a feeling of irrational dread. 'You didn't know that?'

Grace shook her head, sending her blonde hair flying.

'I didn't know.'

How could he? How could Ivan have done such a thing and not told her? He must have known how Constantine's appearance would affect her, the pain it would inflict. Ivan of all people would know how far from being fully healed were the scars of the past, and yet he had behaved in a way that was the emotional equivalent of ripping open the old wounds.

'But believe me, if I had known—if I'd had so much as the faintest suspicion that you might be here—then I wouldn't have come. I would have gone anywhere rather than here—anywhere at all. After the way you behaved, I never wanted to see you again...'

Constantine's beautifully carved mouth twisted in an expression of scorn that was heightened by the flare of fury in the inky depths of his eyes.

'After the way *you* behaved...' he returned silkily '...the feeling is entirely mutual. The question is, where do we go from here?'

'You could turn round and walk out.' Grace made the suggestion with little hope that it would be taken up, her fears confirmed as she saw the uncompromising shake of his dark head. Constantine Kiriazis would have known she must be here, and would have had his strategy worked out well in advance. He had never backed down before anyone. She had never really expected that he was going to start now.

'Then...'

'Gracie?' It was Ivan's voice, coming from very close behind her. 'Are you—? Constantine! You made it! So tell me…how is my favourite Greek tycoon?'

'I am well.'

Grace watched as Constantine submitted to the exuberant hug Ivan gave him with resigned patience. But one dark, straight brow did lift in questioning amazement at the other man's costume of a school uniform, complete with two-coloured cap.

'Ivan, my friend, were you truly still at school ten years ago? I thought that at the age of twenty you were actually at university…'

'Strictly speaking, that's true.' Ivan laughed back. 'But I was much happier at school, so I went for that. And if that's bending the rules, who cares? After all, this is my party, so I can do as I like.'

'Fair enough.' Constantine's amusement was evident in the warmth of his tone. A warmth that had been distinctly lacking when he had talked to her, Grace registered miserably.

This was one of the ways he had surprised her in the past. She had never expected that such a blatantly macho male as Constantine was would ever tolerate her friendship with the other, openly gay man. But Constantine had not only accepted it, he had apparently warmed to Ivan himself too.

In that, at least, he hadn't behaved at all in the way she had expected. But in other ways, she reminded herself bitterly, he had been pure arrogant Greek male through and through. And when that pride had been turned on her it had savaged her life, ripping it apart.

'I wasn't sure if you would make it,' Ivan was saying. 'I thought you might be somewhere the other side of the world.'

As if that would stop Constantine going anywhere he wanted to be. This was a man who used his private plane to fly from country to country with the casual ease that other, lesser mortals might take a bus or the Tube. And wherever he was he always had a fleet of chauffeur-driven cars at his disposal. He had probably expended less effort to get here tonight than Grace herself.

But her thoughts had distracted her from what Constantine was saying. Too late she registered his words with a sense of horrified shock.

'...major problems in the London office. I expect they will take three months or more to sort out.'

No! Grace barely caught back her response before the single word revealed her feelings. The only way she had coped over the past two years was by knowing that Constantine was thousands of miles away, in his office in Athens, or the family home on Skyros. The thought of him being practically on her doorstep for the next few months was a prospect that appalled her.

'So we can hope to see more of you,' Ivan continued, blithely ignoring the look of alarmed appeal Grace shot him. 'Can't be bad. Now, let me relieve you of that *gorgeous* coat.'

But as Constantine shrugged himself out of the elegant garment the sound of a buzzer from the kitchen brought Ivan's platinum blond head swinging round.

'The food! I'm sorry, darlings, I must dash or it will all be ruined. Gracie, you'll see to this for me, won't you?'

And, dumping Constantine's coat in the arms she had no option but to hold out—it was either that or let it fall to the floor—he turned and with an airy wave in their vague direction hurried away again.

'I see Ivan hasn't changed.' Constantine's tone was dry. 'Outrageous as ever.'

'That's Ivan...'

Grace prayed that her response didn't sound as shaken and upset to Constantine as it did in her own ears. She was having to struggle to control the unexpected reaction that had assailed her simply as a result of holding the coat. It felt too personal, somehow, too intimate.

Soft and sensuous, it was still warm from the heat of Constantine's body, and the tangy scent of the cologne he always wore still clung to the material, agonisingly familiar. It was impossible not to recall how in the past, when she had been held close to him, that fragrance had always filled her nostrils, intoxicatingly blended with the more subtle, personal aroma of his body. If she closed her eyes she could still feel the heat of his skin under her fingertips, the brush of his black hair against her cheek...

'Grace?'

Constantine's husky-voiced question intruded into the torrent of sensual memories that had flooded her mind, snapping her back to reality with a painful jolt. Wide and startled, her eyes flew open to clash sharply with his frowning black ones.

'Where did you go?'

'Nowhere!'

Her sharp response was too fast, too spiky, arousing his suspicions instead of subduing them. She saw his dark brows draw together swiftly and hastily set herself to covering her tracks.

'I—I'm just a little tired,' she invented hastily. 'It's been a difficult week at work. We've been having problems with a new campaign...'

'You are still at Henderson and Cartwright?'

'Yes...'

That was better. Her voice was back under control, calm and even.

'I was promoted recently. Now I'm in charge of... But you don't want to know this.'

She didn't want him to know it. She didn't want to let him know anything about her life or what was going on in it. He had relinquished that right when he had turned his back on her, and she had no intention of ever letting him in again.

Constantine's shrug dismissed her comment as irrelevant.

'I thought you were making polite conversation,' he drawled indifferently. 'It is something you are so good at here in England. It is so very civilised, especially in an uncomfortable situation.'

'I'm not uncomfortable!' Grace snapped defensively, grey eyes flashing defiantly.

'Perhaps I meant myself,'

'Oh, that I can't believe!' With a wave of her hand she dismissed Constantine's silky murmur. 'I've never seen you fazed by anything. You wouldn't have got where you are if you let anything get to you. And you've been trained by an expert—your father.'

But she was on dangerous ground there. She knew it from the way his proud head went back sharply, the flare of something menacing in his eyes. But when he spoke no trace of his inner feelings shaded his tone.

'Nevertheless, this could be somewhat...' He hunted for the right word. 'Awkward for you.'

'That's something of an understatement.'

Biting her lip, she wished the careless words back as she realised the advantage she had thoughtlessly given him.

He was quick to pounce on it, of course, that sensual mouth curving into a sardonic smile at her discomfiture.

'You are clearly at a disadvantage here—Ivan gave you no warning of the fact that he had invited me, and I presume that some people here will know what passed between us.'

He knew only too well that almost everyone Ivan had invited would be aware of the fact that two years ago she had been about to marry this man, but that the wedding had never taken place. They might be unclear on the gruesome details, but after that final, appallingly public scene in the foyer of the agency, no one could be in any doubt that Constantine had tossed her aside and walked out of her life, ignoring her pleading for a second chance.

The fact that she had also been at fault in the beginning brought the additional complication of a guilty conscience to an already volatile mixture of emotions roiling inside her. Under the cover of the coat, her hands clenched tightly, crushing the expensive material.

'That was two years ago, Constantine,' she told him coldly. 'Two years in which I have got on with my life, as I presume you have with yours.'

His nod of agreement was curt to the point of rudeness.

'I'm over it,' he declared bluntly.

'And so am I.' Grace wished she could sound as assured as he had done. 'People have short memories. You and I might once have been a nine-day wonder, but now we're stale news. Neither of us can leave—it would upset Ivan too much. So we're just going to have to make the best of things. Don't you agree?'

The look that seared over her was icily assessing; black eyes narrowed thoughtfully for a moment.

'It should be easy enough,' he said at last, his tone a masterpiece of indifference. 'I shall simply do what I have done every day for the past two years, and that is to wipe your existence from my mind, forget I ever met you.'

'In that case, why come here at all? You must have known...'

'Obviously I knew you'd be here, but the wish to please Ivan on his birthday was strong enough to overcome the repugnance I felt at the thought of seeing you again.'

It was meant to hurt, and it achieved its aim with all the ruthless efficiency for which Constantine had achieved his reputation in the business world. Grace was deeply thankful for the protective concealment of the coat she still held as she crushed it close to her, feeling almost as if she needed to stem some agonising internal bleeding that had sprung from the wound he had deliberately inflicted on her.

'But I don't have to spend any more time with you. There are enough people here to distract us...' An autocratic wave of one hand encompassed the crowded room at the far end of the hall. 'And the room is quite large enough to keep us apart for some time.'

'I couldn't agree more.' She had to force herself to say it. 'If we're really lucky, we won't even have to see each other again.'

She would do it if it killed her, would rather die than let him see just what it was doing to her to have him here like this. Constantine nodded slowly, his gaze already drifting away towards the other room where other, obviously more attractive company awaited him.

'That would make it possible to salvage something from this appalling evening.'

'Then don't let me hold you back!'

Her tartness drew that black-eyed gaze back to her for one more of those uncomfortably probing stares, a faintly cynical smile playing around Constantine's firm mouth.

'To be honest, my dear Grace, I sincerely doubt that anything you could do would ever affect me again.'

Was it possible? Grace asked herself as he strolled away without so much as a backward glance. Could he really feel nothing for her, not even the dark anger she had seen blazing in his face at their last, cataclysmic meeting? Did she now mean so little to him that he could dismiss her from his thoughts in the blink of an eye? What had happened to the love he had once declared so eloquently, the passion he had been unable to hide?

It was dead, she told herself drearily, dead and gone, as if it had never existed. Which seemed impossible when her own feelings were in such agonised turmoil that she felt as if there was a raging tornado where her heart should be, a monstrous tidal wave of shock and distress swamping her stomach. She could only pray that she was enough of an actor to hide her misery from Constantine. That she would be able to get through what remained of this evening without giving herself away completely.

CHAPTER TWO

IT WAS impossible.

There was no way at all that she could pretend, even to herself, that she was oblivious to the fact that Constantine was there in the room with her. His presence was like a constant dark shadow, always hovering at her shoulder, following her everywhere she went.

If she paused to talk to anyone she felt him there, just out of sight, driving all thought of what she had been about to say from her mind. If she tried to drink some wine, or taste some food from the extensive buffet Ivan had laid on, her throat closed over what she was trying to swallow, threatening to choke her.

And the worst thing was that, for some private reason of his own, Constantine hadn't kept to his declaration that he was going to wipe her existence from her mind. She had only to glance across the room to meet the intent stare of his watchful black eyes following every movement she made, every smile, every word she spoke.

In the end she sought refuge in the kitchen, privately admitting to her own cowardice as she used the excuse of the mounting pile of washing up to keep her there, hidden away. She was filling the bowl with hot water for the second time when Ivan wandered into the room.

'Uh—oh! I wondered where you'd got to. Does this mean I made a mistake?'

'In inviting Constantine?' Grace turned a reproving look on him. 'What do you think? Ivan, how could you?'

'No chance of you two making it up, then?'

21

'Was that what was in your mind when you asked him here? If that was the case, you couldn't be more wrong. It's over, Ivan, and has been for years.'

'Are you sure? He was pretty keen to accept. I thought perhaps—'

'Well, you thought wrong,' Grace inserted hastily, as much to squash down her own foolishly weak heart as it leapt on an absurd flutter of hope as to disillusion her friend. 'Whatever reasons Constantine had for coming here today, seeing me wasn't one of them. I mean, does he look like a man who can't let me out of his sight?'

'He looks like a man with something on his mind, if you ask me,' Ivan returned, with a nod towards the open door.

Reluctantly Grace followed the direction of his gaze, her eyes fixing immediately on the tall, muscular figure of Constantine leaning against the wall. With a glass in one hand, he had his attention firmly fixed on the woman in front of him. Small and curvaceous, with long dark hair, she was wearing a nurse's uniform with a skirt so indecently short she would never have been allowed on to any hospital ward.

'And what he has on his mind is very definitely not me,' she said, unable to erase the bitterness from her voice.

Her stepsister Paula was dark and petite, she recalled on a wrench of pain at the memory. And Constantine had always admitted to being attracted to small, curvy brunettes, so much so that Grace had never quite been able to understand just what he had been doing with *her*.

'Are you sure?'

'Ivan, *leave* it!' Grace pleaded, unable to take any more.

The words had barely left her lips when Constantine looked up suddenly, deep-set eyes meeting Grace's clouded grey ones. For a fleeting, tormenting moment their gazes locked, and she shivered before the cruel indifference in

their ebony darkness. Then with a cold travesty of a smile
Constantine lifted his glass in a grim mockery of a toast,
one that had her biting down hard on her lower lip to keep
back an expression of pain.

Swinging round so that she no longer had to see him or
his companion, she squirted washing-up liquid into the
bowl with a force that made bubbles boil up wildly.

'Constantine has no thought of any reconciliation on his
mind,' she said through gritted teeth, blinking hard against
the burning tears that stung her eyes. 'Just get that into your
head, will you?'

And just who are you trying to convince? her conscience
questioned reproachfully, distracting her so that she was
barely aware of Ivan leaving her alone again.

Was it true? Was it possible? Had she really been fool
enough to harbour even the faintest hope after all this time?
Oh Grace, Grace! You fool! You crazy, weak-minded fool!

How could she ever have been so stupid? Hadn't
Constantine made his feelings, or rather his lack of them,
brutally clear? Had she spent so many long, lonely nights
lying awake with that final callous dismissal still sounding
in her thoughts, and yet not been convinced by it? She had
to be out of her tiny, crazy mind if that was the case.

We have no future together... The words Constantine
had flung at her, the coldly contemptuous voice in which
they had been spoken lacerated her soul all over again,
making his feelings for her patently clear.

Clear enough even for the most foolish, naively besotted
heart, Grace told herself miserably. In spite of being
blinded by love, as she had been then, she had heard the
conviction in his voice, recognised the finality of the emotional life-sentence he had been handing her. So why
should she allow herself to dare to question it now, when
surely the two years' silence, two years' distance on

Constantine's part, was added evidence of just how much he had meant what he'd said?

'If you wash that plate any more, you will erase the pattern from it.'

The dryly amused voice, instantly recognisable as Constantine's, broke into her reverie with such unexpected suddenness that she started violently, dropping the plate into the washing-up water in a plume of spray.

'Don't sneak up on me like that!'

'I did not sneak. You must have a guilty conscience to jump like that. Or perhaps you were daydreaming. Is that it, *agape mou*? Were you thinking of some man—someone deeply important to you, to judge by the look on your face?'

'I wasn't thinking of anyone!' Grace objected, terrified that he would suspect the true nature of her thoughts. 'And don't call me that! I'm not your love any more!'

'So you remember the Greek I taught you?'

She remembered *that* particular phrase! How could she ever forget it? Her thoughts skittered away from memories too painful to bear. Memories of tenderly embracing in the warm darkness of a mild early spring evening on Skyros, her head pillowed on the strong frame of his chest, hearing that softly accented voice whispering those words in a way that resonated with barely suppressed desire.

'Oh, yes, I remember that, and so many other valuable lessons you taught me.' Grace laced the words with vinegar, deliberately taking them miles away from the sort of lessons he had originally had in mind. 'And believe me, I don't ever intend to forget them. I— What are you doing?'

She flinched back as Constantine moved suddenly, one hand coming out towards her face.

Her instinctive panic earned her a sharp-eyed glance of reproof, Constantine's mouth twisting cynically.

'You have soap bubbles on your nose…' A long finger gently flicked the froth away. 'And on your brow… They might have gone into your eye.'

'Thank you.'

It was muttered ungraciously because she was struggling with the shock waves of sensation, the recollection of other, very different feelings that this man's lightest touch had once sparked off inside her. Times when it had seemed that those long, square-tipped fingers might have been made of molten steel, so intense had been the force of her reaction. She had felt as if the path they had taken was scorched deep into her flesh, branding her irrevocably as his.

'It was no trouble,' Constantine returned, the elaborate courtesy deliberately mocking at her stilted response. 'Would you like some help in here?'

It was the last thing she wanted. Standing so close to her, she was sure he must sense the unevenness of her breathing, hear the heavy pounding of her heart. Just when she most wanted to appear unmoved and totally indifferent to his proximity, her traitorous body seemed determined to go into sensual overdrive, responding to the nearness of his with all the hunger of a famine victim suddenly presented with the most tempting banquet.

'Won't that rather spoil your plan to behave as if I don't exist?' she demanded, hiding her unsettled feelings behind a show of aggression. 'Anyway there's no need. There's nothing left to do.'

To demonstrate the fact she removed the last plate and plonked it down on the drying rack before upending the bowl in the sink so that the soapy water drained away with a faint gurgling sound.

'Then shall I fetch you a drink?'

Nerves on edge, Grace swung round suddenly to glare into Constantine's unreadable black eyes.

'Just what game are you playing now, Constantine? What exactly are you doing here?'

'No game, I assure you. Perhaps a compromise…'

'Compromise!' Grace scoffed. 'I thought such a word didn't exist in your vocabulary. You wouldn't know a compromise if you came face to face with one.'

'I am trying to be reasonable here.' Constantine's careful restraint was obviously slipping slightly, traces of the barely reined in temper escaping his ruthless control. 'I do not feel comfortable being at a party where the woman who is one of the host's best friends spends all her time hiding in the kitchen, especially when I suspect that—'

'Suspect what?' Grace broke in, definitely rattled. 'That you're the reason I'm "hiding" away in here? I always knew your ego was excessively healthy, but…'

'Grace, this *is* meant to be a Turn Back the Clock party. Surely it should be possible for two mature, civilised adults to abide by the theme of tonight.'

'And turn back the clock until when, precisely?'

It was scary to realise how much she wanted to do just that. Frankly terrifying to admit that her heart had leapt in anticipation of the prospect.

If only they could! If only they really could go back to the time when he had been her life and she had believed herself his. The time when they had been so much a couple that they had thought, acted, almost even breathed as one. The time before Paula's lies and her own fears had ripped them apart, driving a chasm between them that it seemed nothing could bridge.

'Well, the idea of the party is that everyone comes as they were ten years ago, but I'm afraid I have problems trying to imagine you at fourteen.'

Constantine's sudden brief flash of a grin was devastating in its impact, winging its way to Grace's already vulnerable heart like an arrow into the gold at the centre of a target. In spite of herself, she couldn't hold back a faint sigh of response, regretting it at once as soon as she saw those brilliant black eyes narrow in swift calculation.

'So what if we settle on half of that time? Five years ago we would have been complete strangers. We'd never even met.'

The faint flame of hope that had lit inside Grace's heart flickered briefly then abruptly went out. If she had needed any warning that their thoughts were running on entirely different lines, then he couldn't have given it more clearly.

Turn back the clock. She had taken that phrase to mean going back to the beginning of their relationship, to the time when their love had been fresh and new, intoxicating in its heady delight. To Constantine, the idea was that they should act as if they had never met, as if they were total strangers to each other.

'All right,' she managed, swallowing down the burning disappointment that seemed to eat at her like acid. 'That should be okay.'

Gravely she held out her hand to him, schooling herself to make sure it showed no betraying tremor.

'I—I'm Grace Vernon. Pleased to meet you.'

Constantine fell in with her pretence with an intuitive ease that made her heart ache with the memory of how it had once been, when that easy understanding had been used on other, far more important matters.

'Constantine Kiriazis,' he replied, taking the offered hand and executing a small formal bow over it. 'Can I get you a drink?'

'W-white wine, please.'

The last thing she wanted was anything alcoholic. Already she felt as if every one of her senses was on red alert, hypersensitive to the sensual force of his physical presence, and she needed no stimulation to add to the sensations that were sizzling through her.

But what she *did* need was a brief time to herself. A few moments in which to draw breath, try to slow the frantic, erratic pulse of her heart. Constantine had only to touch her and she felt as if she had foolishly grabbed at the exposed end of a live electrical cable, violent shocks running up her arm, along every exposed nerve. Instinctively she cradled the hand he had released against her breasts, nursing it as it if had actually been burned.

Just what was he up to? Because he had to be up to something. Less than an hour ago he had declared his intention of ignoring the fact that she was at the party. Now, he was actively seeking out her company.

'White wine…'

Far more quickly than she had anticipated, and certainly long before she was mentally ready, Constantine was back, two glasses in his hands.

'Dry white, of course,' he added with a wry twist to his mouth. 'Though I suppose that technically I shouldn't have known that and should have asked what you'd prefer. This isn't going to be as simple as I thought.'

'Not if we're going to play it strictly by the rules.'

Rules? What rules? Precisely what rules came into play in this sort of situation?

'I think we can allow a little leeway,' Constantine was saying, his words coming dimly through the fog of misery dimming her thoughts. 'After all, I've already asked you about your work, so there's really no need for the "And what do you do?" conversation. One thing I did wonder, though…'

'What was that?' Grace asked, swallowing a much needed sip of the cool, crisp wine, and feeling the effect of the alcohol spread through her body with unnerving rapidity.

She must be much more on edge than she had realised. Better take it steady. Or perhaps her response was to the brilliant smile Constantine had turned on her, and not the wine at all. In that case, she needed to be even more careful. The last thing she wanted was to end up tipsy and not fully in control.

She had to keep a clear mind and all her wits about her if she was to cope with Constantine at his devastating social best. She had seen him turn on the charm so many times, seen far more sophisticated, more blasé personalities melt underneath its potent warmth not to be wary of the powerful spell he could weave with the force of his personality.

'Did you really dress like that when you were fourteen? I find it hard to believe that the elegant Grace Vernon ever deliberately chose to appear in public looking...'

'Such a sight?' Grace finished for him when he seemed uncharacteristically uncertain of how to finish his sentence. 'I think that was the idea.'

In spite of herself a small, wry grin surfaced as she looked into the darkness of his eyes.

'I was rebelling as hard as I could. Going against everything my mother wanted. She insisted on my dressing smartly, as she did. She hated me in trousers, and jeans were anathema to her. So, naturally, I took every opportunity to annoy her by wearing them.'

'Your mother was still married to your father ten years ago?'

'Just. The marriage was already on the rocks, though. She'd already had more than one affair and my father had just met Diana. Mum and Dad separated very soon afterwards.'

'And you went to live with your father. Isn't it more usual for the child to live with her mother?'

'I wasn't exactly a child, Constantine.'

They had never talked about this when they had known each other before. Perhaps if they had things might have been different. He might have understood about Paula. But, no, she couldn't let her thoughts go down that path. It led to too much pain.

'I was old enough to have some say in the matter. I chose to live with my father and, deep down, I'm sure my mother didn't mind. She already had her sights set on a new life in America, and a teenage daughter would just have held her back. My school was here in London, all my friends, naturally I wanted to stay.'

'Even when he married Diana?'

'Even when he married Diana!'

Grace moved to deposit her glass on the worktop with a distinct crash. They were getting into dangerous territory. Talk of Diana led inevitably to thoughts of Paula, her stepmother's daughter.

'I was really happy that he was getting married again. I thought that...'

But she never completed the sentence. At that moment their private haven was invaded by a bunch of laughing, joking party guests.

'Come on, party poopers! You can't stay in here all night! Ivan's going to cut the cake, and he says that instead of it just being him who gets a wish, we can all have one too!'

Grace could only watch and follow as Constantine was led away into the next room, her friends urging her after him. It was as if a sheet of glass had come down between her and the rest of the people in the room. She could see them, hear their voices and their movements, but the sounds were blurred and incomprehensible so that she felt completely cut off from reality.

A wish. If she had been offered a wish by some fairy godmother only a couple of hours ago—less—she would have said that what she wanted most in the world was to make peace with Constantine. That if she could just come to some sort of accord with him, it would be enough to satisfy her. She had truly believed that if they could come to an understanding where they could be on civilised terms, she could be content.

But they had achieved that truce, those civilised terms, and all that it had taught her was that it was *not enough*. It could never be enough. She didn't want *peace* with Constantine; she didn't want *civilised*. She wanted so much more.

'Happy birthday, dear Ivan...'

All around her Ivan's guests joined in the traditional singing of 'Happy Birthday', and Grace forced herself to open and close her mouth along with them. But no words would form, her tongue seeming to have frozen, her lips as stiff as board.

There was no backing away from it. No avoiding the realisation that had hit her hard, like the splash in her face. The two intervening years might as well have not existed. They had had no effect on the way she was feeling. No effect at all.

'Grace?'

'W-what?'

Somehow she dragged her thoughts out of the shocked daze in which they were hidden, forcing her eyes to focus on the man who had come to her side.

Constantine. Hastily she veiled her eyes, hiding her feelings behind her lids, her heart jerking into a rapid, jolting beat at the thought that he might be able to read what was in her mind. The cake-cutting ceremony was over, and the party had moved on, the pulsing music starting up again.

'Dance with me?'

Say no! Every instinct screamed the warning at her, every nerve instantly thrown into panic mode. Say no—back away—just turn—run! Anything other than expose her already weakened defences to the potent onslaught of his sensual appeal. She already knew how vulnerable she was to the sight, the sound, the scent of him. How her body reacted to just the slightest touch. She couldn't risk...

'Yes, okay.'

How had that happened? Just what was she doing? Grace could find no answers for her outraged sense of self-preservation. She was acting on a far deeper, more primitive level, responding purely on instinct, unable to force her mind into any form of rational thought.

So she let Constantine take her hand and draw her towards the part of the room that had been cleared for dancing. And when the music changed just as they started to dance, turning from a rhythmic beat to a slow, seductive number, she made no objection to the way he turned to her and took her into his arms, drawing her close to the warmth and strength of his body.

She fitted into his arms as if she'd been born there. And it felt like coming home. The rest of the room, the noise and all the people around her, blurred into one indecipherable mass. There was no one in the world but herself and this man, whose strength enclosed her, whose heart beat under her cheek, the strong wall of his chest rising and falling with every breath he took.

'Grace...' he murmured softly, her name just a sigh against her hair.

'Don't talk...' Grace heard herself whisper back. 'Just hold me...'

She had no idea whether it was simply one dance that seemed to last for ever, or if there were many such dances, impossible to count, while she was lost in a dreamy haze of sensual delight. She only knew that when at last the music faded into silence and the world around her righted itself again she was no longer in the big main room where the party was centred, but had been subtly manoeuvred out into the hall beyond.

'Where...?' she began in confusion.

As her eyes focused again she discovered that she and Constantine were in the shelter of the wide flight of stairs up to the next floor, hidden from everyone.

Immediately the dream world that had enclosed her vanished, evaporating swiftly like a mist before the sun. Reality came rushing back with a speed and force that rocked her on her feet, made her shiver convulsively.

'What are we doing here? I can't—'

'Grace...' Constantine silenced her by laying strong tanned fingers across her mouth. 'I want some time alone with you.'

'You!'

Grace wrenched her head away from the gentle pressure of his hand, grey eyes blazing up into his black ones, seeing the way that the heavy lids came down over them, concealing his feelings from her.

'You want! You *want*! Isn't that always the way with you? What you want comes before everything else. "Dance with me..."'

Deliberately she mimicked his own words of earlier, emphasising the autocratic note, the lack of any 'please' that had turned the phrase into a command rather than a request.

'"I want some time alone with you."'

'I got the impression that was what you wanted too.'

'And how, precisely, did you come to that conclusion?'

Constantine's proud head bent until his mouth was level with her ear, and his voice was softly husky, his warmth breath caressing her skin as he whispered, '"Don't talk... Just hold me."'

His echoing of her own foolish reaction was uncannily accurate, making her head go back in shock.

Had she really been so stupid? Had she really let her feelings get the better of her? Had she been so weak as to put that pleading note into her voice, the one that Constantine had just reproduced with merciless exactness? How could she have betrayed herself in that way?

'I—I was enjoying the dance,' she blustered frantically, desperately trying to cover her tracks. 'But that doesn't mean I wanted anything more.'

'No?'

The lazy lifting of one dark brow questioned the truth of her spluttered declaration.

'You must forgive me if I don't believe—'

'You can believe or not as you want!' Grace tossed back at him, ignoring the ominous thread of warning that shaded the softly accented voice. 'I don't care. I know my own mind, and I don't want anything more to do with you! As a matter of fact, what I really want right now is to go home.'

'Then I will take you,' Constantine returned smoothly.

'No!'

That was definitely not what she had in mind. Desperately she shook her head, so that her fair hair flew out wildly.

'I can make my own way home. It's just a short walk.'

'You no longer live with your father?'

'No.'

Living at home would have meant living with Paula, and that was something neither of them could have handled.

'I have my own place now—about ten minutes away from here. I can walk.'

'And I will escort you.'

Grace groaned inwardly. She knew this mood of old. When Constantine set his mind on something like this, he was immoveable. A dog with a bone had nothing on him. But she couldn't give in to him. If she did, then he would only take it as evidence that his own interpretation of events was the real one.

And wasn't it? her own unforgiving conscience threw at her, refusing to let her off the hook, no matter how much she mentally squirmed. Hadn't she admitted to herself that she wanted...'

But what she wanted and what was *safe* were two very different things. She might dream of more time with Constantine, of letting him know her feelings for him, but to do any such thing would be emotional suicide.

Whatever feelings he might once have had for her, they were obviously now all dead. All, that was, except for the burning sexual attraction that had once flared between them, and which time had not dimmed at all. Weakly, stupidly, she had let Constantine see that it was still there, and with characteristic opportunism he had decided to turn that fact to his advantage.

'Grace, I have never in my life let a woman walk home alone at this time of night. I don't intend to start now. Get your coat. I am coming with you.'

'Do I have any choice?' Wearily she accepted that, short of creating the sort of scene that would have everyone at the party talking for weeks to come, she had no option but to do as he said.

'None at all,' Constantine returned on a note of satisfaction that sounded rich as a tiger's purr. 'I know that we've only just met, but I must insist that you humour me in this.'

Only just met. What...?

It took Grace a moment or two to realise exactly what Constantine meant.

Grace, this is meant to be a Turn Back the Clock party. His words sounded inside her head like a lifeline as she went reluctantly to fetch her coat from the bedroom. *Five years ago we would have been complete strangers.*

So Constantine was still playing according to the rules they had laid down earlier that evening. They were still pretending that they were complete strangers who had met for the first time tonight.

That being so, perhaps she could cope with letting him take her home after all. Surely even Constantine wouldn't pounce on what was supposedly their very first meeting?

It was little enough comfort, but it was all that she had. And Constantine wasn't about to back down, so she could only pray that it was enough.

CHAPTER THREE

'Over there.'

Grace lifted a finger to point, then immediately dropped it again when her hand showed a worrying tendency to shake in a way that revealed her inner turmoil.

'It's the last house on the right. The one with the blue door.'

Constantine's nod of acknowledgement was curt and silent as he steered the car to a halt precisely opposite the door she had indicated. Perhaps, like her, he was already regretting the impulse that had pushed him to insist on taking her home. Perhaps he too had found what stiff and hesitant conversation there had been during the brief journey so uncomfortable that he was glad their time together was almost over.

Which suited Grace fine. All she wanted was to get out of the car and get inside, into the safety and privacy of her small flat. If she had to sit next to Constantine for a moment longer, listen to his stilted, one-word responses to the few remarks she had managed to force herself to make, she was going to scream with frustration.

'That's perfect. Thank you.'

Already she was fumbling with the seatbelt, even before the powerful vehicle had fully come to a halt at the side of the kerb, anxious to be out of the car and away from his unsettling presence.

'It was kind of you to see me home... What did you say?'

The question was jolted from her in response to something Constantine had muttered. Something incomprehensible in Greek that had sounded rough and impatient, still-ing her nervous movements suddenly.

But even as she asked the question, she saw the change in his mood. With an obvious effort he smoothed away the frown that had drawn his brows, the cynical twist to his carved mouth.

'I'll see you to your door,' he said, his voice retaining nothing of the disturbing intonation of moments before.

'There's no need.'

But she was talking to thin air. Already Constantine was out of the car and moving round to open the passenger door for her.

It was only a few yards from the edge of the kerb to the threshold of her house. Just a few short steps, but they seemed to take an eternity, every sound of their feet on the pavement ringing unnaturally loudly in the midnight silence of the street. At her side, Constantine was a dark, silent figure, his long stride outstripping hers so that she had to hurry to keep up with him.

To her intense annoyance she found that her inner tension had communicated itself to her hands, so that she fumbled clumsily as she tried to insert her key in the lock. Supremely conscious of Constantine's eyes, dark as the night sky, watching every awkward move, she cursed herself silently under her breath, trying again. Luckily this time she succeeded, and turned back to face him, relief evident in her smile and her voice.

'Well, here I am. Safe and sound, as you can see. Thank you again for seeing me home.'

If this really had been a first meeting, she would have added something about having enjoyed her evening, per-haps even a suggestion that they could do it again some time. But of course the idea that they could turn back the clock in that way was a pure fiction, throwing her mind into total confusion as she hunted for a way to say goodbye that fitted the circumstances.

'I—I'll say goodnight, then.'

'Is that all?'

'All? You— I mean, what else is there? After all...' She aimed for flippancy and missed it by a mile, her voice becoming high-pitched and shrill. 'We've only just met tonight.'

'So would it be too forward to ask for a kiss goodnight?'

The question sounded light, friendly even. The way he'd been earlier in the evening, in the kitchen, when they'd been pretending that they really had just met.

A goodnight kiss; nothing more. She could cope with that.

But underneath all the carefully rational, logical reasoning lay something darker, something more disturbing. Something that lurked like the jagged rocks at the bottom of a still, calm sea, just waiting to catch at the base of her thinking and rip it apart, laying open the real truth. The one she hardly dared acknowledge to herself. The fact that she wanted this, wanted Constantine's kiss more than she would ever admit.

'Okay.' She nodded—casually, she hoped. 'One kiss goodnight...'

Constantine's head lowered, blocking out the light from the nearby streetlamp, and instinctively her lips parted slightly.

But it was her cheek that his mouth made contact with, the kiss brushing against it warm and soft and so painfully familiar. And heartbreakingly brief.

'Goodnight.'

Before she even had time to think, even as she was steadying herself for the real kiss, the one her lips were aching for, the one that had already quickened her heartbeat in anticipation, he had stepped back.

'Goodnight,' he said again, his voice harsh and flippantly dismissive. 'See you around.'

Grace couldn't believe it. She shivered inside as pain, raw and cruel, ripped through her, lacerating her heart. She had actually let herself believe—had hoped… Bitter tears of humiliation burned in her eyes, blinding her.

'G-goodnight.'

She forced herself to say it. Forced herself to turn the handle and open her door. Felt the rush of warm air from the hall out into the coldness of the night.

But she couldn't make herself step over the threshold and into the house. Even now she couldn't turn and move away from him.

It was *not enough*! She wanted more, so much more. That one kiss had sparked off all the need, the hunger, the passion she had once felt for this man and which she had thought was safely buried, out of sight.

But it seemed that Constantine had spoken nothing more or less than the truth when he had said so casually, 'I'm over it.'

'I—I'll…'

Go! Her mind screamed at her. Out of here *now*, before it gets any worse!

But, *no*, her heart pleaded. Let me have just a little bit more. Just one moment longer in his company. After these two long, empty years, let me have one more chance to hear his voice, see him smile.

Before she knew she had even formed the thought she had acted impulsively. The aroma of Constantine's cologne and the warm, clean scent of his body reached her nostrils as she leaned towards him, making her head swim with the force of its sensual impact. His eyes were deeper, darker pools in the shadows of the night, and she could hear the soft, regular sound of his breathing.

'Goodnight,' she said on a very different note as, taking

her cue from him, she pressed her lips to the hard, lean plane of his cheek. The warm satin of his skin was slightly roughened by the result of a day's growth of beard that brushed abrasively against her mouth.

'And thank you...'

But that one unthinking act proved her undoing. With a phenomenal speed of reaction, Constantine turned his head so that her lips were forced to move. Unable to do anything but slip over the bronzed skin, as if on ice over a frozen pond, they found themselves sliding inexorably towards the heated softness that was his mouth.

'Grace...'

He muttered something thick and rough in Greek against her lips before taking them harshly, urgently, crushing her mouth under his.

'You should have gone—headed for safety—while you had the chance. Now it's much too late.'

Too late! Grace echoed inside her head on a note of disbelief. It had already been too late in the moment that he'd kissed her. Even such a desultory peck on the cheek had told her all she needed to know.

No, it had been earlier than that. It had happened in the moment when she had opened Ivan's door and looked into the black depths of his eyes and known that, no matter what had happened, Constantine was still the only man in the world for her.

'Sweet Grace...'

A cold sneaking wind wound itself around Grace's legs, but she was beyond noticing it. The bulk of Constantine's strong body protected her from the cold, and the heated race of her blood through her own veins warmed her skin until she felt as if she was on fire. Her heartbeat was staccato with excitement, the coming and going of air in her lungs feverishly erratic.

'You really *should* have gone in.' Constantine's

breathing was every bit as uneven as her own, his voice hoarse and jerky. 'Now there's no turning back. Grace, *agape mou*...invite me in.'

Invite me in. It was a command, not a request. She knew exactly what was behind it, what was uppermost in his mind.

So why wasn't she saying no? Why wasn't she telling him to get out of there and out of her life? The thought slid into her mind very briefly, but then, just as swiftly, slid straight out again.

'D-do...?'

Her voice failed her, drying painfully, so that she had to moisten her lips before she could speak again. In the light from the hall she saw Constantine's black eyes drop to her mouth, to follow the tiny, unconsciously provocative movement with an intensity that made her heart jerk convulsively against her chest.

'Do you want to come in?'

'*Do* I...?' It was a shaken, husky laugh. 'Grace, I swear to God that if you don't let me in with you right now, I'll—'

'There's no need for that!' Grace broke in hurriedly, shaken, breathless, half terrified of what he might be about to say. 'Come in, out of the cold.'

It seemed to her that the slam of the door behind her, shutting out the world and closing them in together, was a sound of decision, defining a moment that would change her life for ever. It was now too late to go back, to even think of changing her mind.

And she didn't want to. All she wanted was right here, with her, at her side. His arms enclosed her. His heart beat under her cheek, and she felt as if she had come home.

But once inside the mood changed sharply. She had barely closed the door before Constantine released her so abruptly that she felt as if she had been dropped from a great height, landing, stunned and disbelieving, on a very hard floor.

She could only watch as he pushed his way into her flat and prowled around it like some caged wild beast, scenting out the borders of its new territory.

Slowly, deliberately, he turned on his heels so that his dark-eyed gaze could take in the comfortable living room with the pale cream armchairs—the room was too small to take a settee—peach velvet curtains, and softly polished pinewood dresser. On the far wall, opposite the big bay window, was a Victorian style cast-iron open fireplace set in a tiled surround.

'It's not very big...' he murmured at last, his survey completed.

'It's all I could afford!' Grace protested indignantly. 'We can't all have homes on every continent and a private plane to ferry us between them.'

'Half of the houses are owned by my parents,' Constantine pointed out, his tone coolly reasonable. 'I only have the use of them.'

'But what you do own my poky little flat would fit into a hundred times over.'

'Did I say it was poky?' he murmured smoothly, continuing his exploration.

He didn't need to, Grace was forced to reflect, ruing her foolish tongue. What she had really meant was that now she saw him in her flat it was as if his tall, imposing presence so dominated the room that it appeared it had shrunk around him, becoming impossibly small and claustrophobic.

'W-would you like coffee?' Belatedly she remembered her role as hostess.

'No.'

Stark and uncompromising, it was tossed over his shoulder at her as he studied the collection of paperbacks on her bookshelf.

'Tea, then?'

'No...'

'Something stronger?'

The question was high-pitched and uneven, coming from a throat that had tightened uncomfortably over the question she knew she was really asking. This was his opportunity to say no, he couldn't drink any more because he was driving.

'Some wine, perhaps?'

An autocratic gesture dismissed the question; Constantine's attention was still fixed on her book collection. But then a moment later he shook his dark head.

'Perhaps—yes...'

'Oh, for heaven's sake, Constantine!' Grace exploded, more on edge than she had allowed herself to admit. 'Yes—no—perhaps... Which is it?' she added, braving his swift frown. 'Make up your mind.'

'*Cristos*, I am trying to be civilised, that is all! But I feel—'

'You feel?' Grace echoed when he broke off abruptly. 'What do you feel?'

Unexpectedly those black eyes avoided her questioning grey ones. It was such a shock to see the confident, self-assured Constantine Kiriazis so uncharacteristically at a loss for words that it gave her the determination to go on, push him a little harder.

'Constantine? What do you feel?'

For the space of another heartbeat he still hesitated. But then, just when she was sure he was going to ignore her completely, or change the subject, a dismissive lift of the broad shoulders under the elegant coat shrugged off whatever restraint he was imposing on himself.

'I feel totally uncivilised,' he muttered, his voice thickened and rough. 'If you want the truth, I feel wild, pagan—primitive.'

Well, she'd asked!

'And why…?'

'You know why!'

Constantine flung the words at her as if he hated having to speak them. Yellow flames of emotion flared in his eyes, burning away the control he had been imposing so ruthlessly up until this moment, and his proud head went back in a gesture of defiance.

'I feel this way because of you. I *want* you! I've wanted you all night! I've always wanted you—and I doubt if I'll ever be cured of this need. The two years we've been apart have been hell. Not having you has been like an ache in my gut, always there, always reminding me of how it used to be.'

'Me?'

She couldn't believe what she had heard. It wasn't a declaration of love, but right now it was enough. He wanted her. He had missed her. He had hurt being without her.

'Grace.'

Her name was a raw, rough-voiced sound.

'Grace, come here!'

Common sense screamed at her to be careful, to hesitate, to allow time for second thoughts. But her heart brushed aside such foolish considerations impatiently.

She wasn't even aware of having moved before she was across the room and in his arms, feeling them close around her, holding her tight.

His mouth claimed hers in the same second, shocking in its wild, hungry demand. And Grace responded in kind, all the pent-up longing, the loneliness, the agony of the past two years exploding into a white-hot, raging conflagration of need. She kissed him back with all the force of her emotions laid bare for him to see.

'Grace, *pethi mou*…beautiful Grace…' Constantine muttered against her mouth. 'You are mine. You always have been mine. I will let no one else…'

'There is no one else,' Grace managed breathlessly, dragging in air in a brief respite from the calculated assault upon her senses. 'No one now, no one—'

Some sixth sense had her snatching back the final word before she spoke it. She wanted Constantine to know that there was no other man in her life right now. Whether she also wanted to admit that there had been no one else since he had walked out on her was quite another matter entirely.

Oh, there had been plenty of interest. She had even been out on a few dates. But they had been short and not particularly sweet. No matter how hard she'd tried, she'd found it impossible to put on even a show of an interest she was very far from feeling.

And now she knew why. For the past two years she had been slowly starving inside, wasting away emotionally without a sight or sound of Constantine to nourish her. She had been in suspended animation, like Sleeping Beauty, waiting only for his kiss to bring her alive again.

And she never wanted to go back to those empty days. Never wanted even to think of them. Particularly not now, with Constantine's arms enclosing her, his hands caressing her body, his mouth following a heated trail from her lips, across the soft skin of her cheek and down her throat to where her heightened pulse beat frantically in the scooped neckline of her tee shirt.

'I lied, you know…' he muttered against her hot skin.

'What?'

Adrift on a warm sea of pleasure, Grace only registered that he had spoken. But then the true import of that *lied* hit home, slashing into her delirium.

'You *what*?' Fear clutched at her heart. 'Constantine?'

His laughter feathered over her tightly stretched nerves, softly reassuring.

'I lied. When I said I didn't like what you were wearing.'

'"Distressingly unflattering" were the words you used, I believe,' Grace managed, the words sounding strangled and uneven as long-fingered bronzed hands smoothed over the offending outfit, making her writhe in responsive delight.

'Distressingly *provocative* is more like it!' Constantine growled. 'Do you know what it does to me to see the way those jeans hug your pert little backside, the sway of your breasts underneath your tee shirt?'

'I never wore a bra when I was fourteen.'

Her reply broke in the middle, cracking noticeably as those wickedly knowing fingers found the small gap between the bottom of her shrunken tee shirt and the tight-fitting waistband of the denim jeans. Shuddering in response to the tiny electric shocks of pleasure his touch sparked off along her sensitised nerves, she caught her lower lip between her teeth in order to hold back the cry of delight that almost escaped her.

'And every time you moved, this tiny patch of skin could just be seen…tormenting me, tantalising, just begging to be touched.'

He was touching it now—with a vengeance! Making her shiver and writhe against him in a way that made the heated force of his desire only too obvious through the fine fabric of his well-cut trousers. Her blood raced through her veins, making her heart pound, her thoughts swim.

'Grace…'

'No. Shh!'

Gently she silenced him by laying soft fingers over his mouth, stilling what he had been about to say.

'No words—for now.'

There had been too many words between them in the

past. Hurtful, destructive words that had shattered the love they had once shared, smashing it into tiny pieces.

'Don't talk. Let's just let our lips…'

She kissed him softly on the forehead, the bridge of his nose, the burning eyes that closed under the gentle caress.

'Our hands…'

Her fingertips slid through the silky black hair, down over the strong muscles cording his neck, and under the soft cashmere of his coat. With only a little urging she was able to lift it and slide it from the powerful shoulders, letting it fall in a heavy pool on the floor at their feet.

'And our bodies do the talking.'

Deliberately she inched closer, circling her pelvis over his, a teasing smile curling her lips as she heard the groan of response he could not hold back.

'Lips, hands and bodies… Suits me.'

With a rough, husky laugh deep in his throat, he echoed her own movements, sliding the leather jacket from her shoulders, down her arms, and discarding it somewhere, tossing it disdainfully aside without caring where it fell.

His mouth was everywhere, on her face, her throat, tugging at the scooped neck of her tee shirt in order to gain access to the soft, sensitive skin of her shoulders. And his hands trailed paths of fire under the white cotton, across the slender contours of her waist, the fine bones of her ribcage, and slowly, irresistibly upwards, towards the aching, waiting peaks of her breasts.

When she had dreamed of it so often, longed for it so many times in the loneliness of the past years, the feel of the heat of his palms against her sensitised flesh was so devastating that she twisted against him, shaken by the convulsions of sensual need that sizzled through her fine-boned frame like lightning across a storm-dark sky. And lower down, deep at the most feminine core of her being, an answering pulse of hunger began to throb in a primal, basic rhythm that would allow for only one possible appeasement.

'This will have to go...'

Constantine wrenched the white tee shirt from her with such force that she heard the worn material rip. But she couldn't bring herself to spare the abused garment more than the briefest passing thought as it too was discarded, Constantine's strong brown fingers caressing her skin, leaving her no time to feel cold.

'And these...'

As he dealt with her belt and the clasp at her waist with brusque efficiency, his hot mouth seemed to everywhere on the upper part of her body, kissing, licking, nibbling, even taking tiny playful nips at her skin that didn't hurt but only fuelled the spiralling storm of hunger roiling up inside her.

She wanted Constantine every bit as much as he had made clear that he wanted her. She felt that she would die if he didn't make love to her, right here and now, without a thought for the future or their unhappy past. Without Constantine she *had* no future. The present, this room, this man, and the wild electrical storm he had sparked off inside her were all that had any reality for her.

'The bedroom...'

Constantine's voice was thick and rough in her ear, and as she struggled to focus on his carved face she saw the febrile glitter in his eyes, the streak of burning colour along the broad cheekbones that betrayed how close he was to losing control completely.

She had barely time to make a wild gesture vaguely in the right direction before she was snatched off her feet and carried bodily across the room. Constantine kicked open the door, crossing the oatmeal-coloured carpet in three swift strides before depositing her on the cream cotton of the duvet cover with scant ceremony. She had scarcely time to draw in a ragged, uneven breath before he came down beside her on the bed.

'Undress me, Grace,' he ordered. 'I want to be naked, like you. I want to feel your skin against mine.'

It was what she wanted too. Wanted with an urgency that made her fingers clumsy, driving her to fumble with the buttons on his shirt, impatient tears stinging her eyes as she made a complete hash of the simple task.

'Here...' Long fingers stilled her increasingly frantic attempts. 'Let me.'

In just a few seconds the shirt and waistcoat were stripped from his strong body, his trousers following with equally swift efficiency, and when he came back to her again he was totally, proudly nude, completely unselfconscious and blatantly, magnificently aroused.

'Now,' he said, sliding his long body down on the soft cotton beside her. 'Now we can do this properly.'

Pushing her back against the pillows, he subjected her to a sensual onslaught that made the breath catch in her throat in a strangled moan of hungry pleasure. There wasn't an inch of her quivering body that he didn't kiss, the tiniest spot on her burning skin that didn't feel the calculated caress of his knowing hands. His lips were like fire on her breasts, blazing a trail to the tight, stinging nipples and closing over first one and then the other, toying softly before suckling hard, sending shafts of white-hot fire searing down the nerves between her thighs.

Muttering in a mixture of agonised delight and screaming tension, Grace couldn't keep her own hands still. She wanted to touch him anywhere, everywhere, her fingers clutching, stroking, skimming over every part of the powerful body she could reach.

One moment they tangled in the black silk of his hair, another they were smoothing the taut, straining muscles of his shoulders and back. And then, as excitement made her bolder, they slid between their bodies and explored the soft dark hair that curled at the base of his erection, the hot, hard shaft itself.

'*Theos*, Grace!' Constantine muttered thickly. 'You are like wildfire—so hot—so eager! You never used to be so responsive.'

Never used to be... No, in the past she had had foolish, naive ideas that clinging on to her virginity mattered more than showing how she felt about this man. She had wanted everything. The perfect wedding, church flowers—and to be the virgin bride as well!

And as a result of wanting everything, she had very nearly lost everything too. But not now. Now she had been given this unexpected second chance, and she intended to take it. Grasp it with both hands and never let it go.

'Grace, I need to know something...are you protected?'

'Protected?'

Grace's teeth worried at her bottom lip as she struggled to find a way to answer him. But Constantine needed no words, she realised, as she felt his immediate withdrawal and the obvious cooling of the heated passion that had gripped him.

'I don't—' he began, but she couldn't let him finish.

'And do you think I care?' she cried sharply. 'It *will* be safe, Constantine. It's the wrong time of the month for it not to be. And don't you dare think of stopping now!'

'Grace, I'm not sure...'

'But I am!'

She had never been more sure of anything. Never wanted anything so much in all her life. Constantine had said that wanting her was like an ache in his gut, but he had gravely underestimated the truth. What she felt wasn't so much an ache as a sharp, burning pain of need. Every inch of her body craved his like a drug to which she had become addicted but had been denied for far too long. She felt she would die if he left her alone now.

And so she writhed against Constantine's long, hard body, shifting her slim legs in an invitation that was more blatant than anything she could say.

'Don't talk, Constantine!' she whispered against the coil of his ear. 'You promised action, not words.'

His groan was a sound of surrender, of excitement, of delight, all blended as one. And as his mouth took her lips hard once more, those tantalising hands slipped lower, smoothing over the flat plane of her stomach before sliding between her legs, stroking the soft skin of her inner thighs.

'Action? Like this?' he whispered as his sure touch found the most feminine spot of all and caressed it gently.

The choked cry that escaped her was the only response Grace was capable of making, and she clutched him to her, fingers digging into the hard muscles at his shoulders as she arced her body up to meet his in yearning hunger. The need for him now was like a scream inside every nerve, the sexual hunger he had awoken sharp as a pain deep inside.

'Or like *this*?'

The final moment of possession, the fierce, wild thrust of his body into hers, was so much what she wanted that her head swam in a delirium of pleasure. But at the same time some small, residual instinct she couldn't control made her stiffen faintly underneath him, halting him suddenly, his head going back in shock, glazed black eyes staring down into her wide grey ones.

'Still?' he managed, in a tone that left her in no doubt as to his state of mind.

Forcing herself into some degree of consciousness in order to face that appraising stare, Grace managed to move her shoulders in what she hoped was a careless shrug.

'It doesn't matter.' And then, when he remained frozen

into immobility above her, 'It *doesn't matter*, Constantine!' she repeated more forcefully, moving her hips under his with deliberate, calculated provocation.

'Grace...' Constantine began, but another of those sensual movements took whatever he had been about to say from his tongue and turned it instead into a groan of ecstatic surrender. The shock in his eyes turned to a glittering hunger *'Grace!'* he sighed on a very different note as he shifted slightly, thrust almost gently.

With that first movement all the careful, almost brutal control he had been exerting splintered, shattering into tiny, irreparable pieces. As one they gave in to the fierce primal rhythm, slowly at first, then faster, faster, faster. Together they clung closer, clutched tighter, reached higher and higher.

To each powerful thrust Grace returned a response of her own, passion answering passion, heat building on heat, harder, fiercer, wilder. Until at last, with the force and starburst brilliance of an exploding meteor, they broke free of the last bonds holding them in time and soared into the formless, dazzling dimension of ecstasy.

Still clinging to Constantine's sweat-slicked form, hearing the breath rasp into his lungs, the shuddering of his muscles as he returned, unwillingly, to reality, Grace could neither think nor feel. She was only aware of the pounding of her heart, still sounding like thunder inside her head, the lingering aftershocks of pleasure that sizzled through her, growing slowly, gradually fainter as a languid sense of repleteness moved along her veins like warm, thick honey.

Stirring slowly, Constantine rolled away from her to lie at her side on the rumpled covers. With a deep, contented sigh, he half opened heavy-lidded eyes, stretching indolently, lazily luxuriating in his own satisfaction.

'I knew it would be like this,' he muttered thickly. 'Knew you...'

'Knew I what?' Grace asked when his voice trailed off.

But Constantine's eyes had already closed, sleep claiming him even as she lifted her head to watch.

Her sigh exactly matching his in deep gratification, Grace shrugged off the momentary confusion.

It didn't matter. Nothing mattered, she told herself as, with an effort, she pulled up the quilt to cover them both before nestling down into the warmth of Constantine's totally relaxed body.

For two years she had lived a sort of half-life, going through the motions, acting on autopilot, putting one foot in front of the other, eating, sleeping, breathing, because she had to. But at the centre of that life there had been an empty core, big and dark as a black hole, taking the real meaning out of living because Constantine was not there.

But now he was back in her life. He was here, beside her, in her bed. He had just made her his finally and completely, by making love to her with the sort of mind-blowing passion that spoke so eloquently of how he must feel. Perhaps they still had a long way to go, but they would travel that road together, and she had no doubt that together they'd reach the happiness she had once been so sure of.

Constantine was back, she repeated inwardly, a blissful smile curling her lips as heavy waves of sleep rolled over her, claiming her. Constantine was back and so everything was right in her world.

CHAPTER FOUR

THE shrill sound of the alarm clock broke violently into the deep, deep sleep that enclosed Grace, jolting her roughly into wakefulness. Groaning wearily, she pushed a hand through her hair, brushing it back from her face so that she could see the clock on her bedside table.

'Seven thirty!' It couldn't be. It still felt like the middle of the night.

But then she had not exactly had a normal night's rest!

It was impossible to hold back a small, contented smile as she recalled just how she had spent the hours of darkness. Her softened eyes went to the side of the bed where Constantine had lain, one hand smoothing over the pillow that still bore the imprint of his dark head, the faint scent of his body.

The end of the night had been a long time coming. They might have dozed, but that first frantic coming together had only temporarily appeased Constantine's appetite for her, and hers for him. He had soon woken again, waking her in her turn with enticing kisses and caresses.

She had lost count of the number of times they had reached for each other, satiation fading into interest, interest sparking into hunger all over again. So that now, as she stretched wearily, she found that her body ached in unexpected places, and there were tiny tender spots to prove that the force and urgency of her lover's desire had been totally unrestrained.

Her lover. Just to frame the words inside her head made her mouth curve into a dreamy, cat-that-got-the-cream

55

smile. Constantine was her lover. He had come back to her, and, to prove it, he had made love to her all night long.

But he was not at her side, where she had expected him to be. His half of the bed was empty, though still warm from the heat of his body. Blinking dreamily, she managed to focus enough to realise that Constantine had slipped from the bed and was quietly hunting for his discarded clothes.

'What are you doing?' Still only half awake, she found it a struggle to force the words out.

Constantine's dark head swung in her direction, his hands still busy with the buttons on his shirt.

'Places to go; people to see.'

His response was curt, almost sharp, certainly totally un-loverlike, so that Grace frowned in sleepy petulance.

'At this time of day!'

'At any time of day. I have a breakfast meeting first thing—a meeting I cannot possibly attend wearing the clothes I had on last night. Then at nine I have to—'

'Okay, okay, I get the message!'

Realising from the impatient way he stamped his feet into his shoes that she was using quite the wrong approach, she hurriedly changed tack completely.

'It's just that I'm disappointed,' she murmured in a soft, enticing tone, accompanying the words by a sensual wriggle of her body under cover of the downy quilt. 'I had thought we could wake up together...start the day properly.'

'Grace!' The look he slanted at her was partly amused, partly reproving, and tinged with what she fervently hoped was a strong thread of regret. 'I am in England to work, remember.'

'Oh, yes,' Grace sighed disconsolately. 'The problems at the London office.'

She should be thankful for them, really. After all, weren't they what had brought Constantine back to her so unexpectedly? But right now she didn't feel at all thankful. All she knew was that her bed was starting to feel very cold and empty, and the man who could remedy that situation was now heading for her sitting room in search of the coat he had discarded all those passion-filled hours ago.

'The problems at the London office,' he confirmed, coming back into the room even as he shrugged himself into the expensive garment that seemed to have suffered no ill effects from its night on her lounge floor. 'They're what I came here to deal with, I never expected to get...sidetracked in this way.'

His glance at his watch was swift, impatient, telling its story only too clearly. Grace knew him in this mood. Determined, unyielding, his mind totally fixed on the matter in hand; there would be no moving him, however hard how she tried.

She might as well give in now in order to avoid any unpleasantness.

'All right, so you have to go. But when will I see you again?'

'I could be tied up all day...'

He moved to drop a kiss on her sleep-flushed cheek. But his lips had barely made contact with her skin before he was straightening up again, checking his watch once more.

'I'll call you.'

'I'll look forward to that...' Grace began, but the words faded from her tongue as he strode from the room, only acknowledging her with a vague gesture of his hand.

It hadn't been the sort of awakening she had anticipated, Grace reflected as she forced herself to go through the everyday motions of showering, dressing, preparing for work. That particular daydream had involved a long, slow start to the morning, with Constantine's arms around her, his mouth pressing kisses all over her face.

But all the same it had been a much better beginning

than she had ever imagined. Constantine was here, back in her life—in her bed—and she couldn't be happier. Just the thought of it was enough to make her feel like dancing as she made her journey to work.

'Someone looks as if all their birthdays have come at once,' Ivan commented when he stopped by her desk later that morning. 'Could this have anything to do with a certain tall, dark, devastating Greek who took you home from the party last night?'

'You know it has!' Grace smiled. 'After all, wasn't that exactly what you had planned right from the start?'

'What I *hoped*,' her friend corrected. 'But only if it's right for you. I wouldn't want you hurt again, Gracie, not like you were the last time.'

'Constantine isn't going to hurt me. When he left this morning he promised he'd ring me tonight and... Oh!'

Her hands flew up to cover her burning cheeks as Ivan's exaggeratedly rounded eyes told her just what she had given away.

'When he left this morning!' he echoed archly. 'Gracie, sweetie, are you sure about this?'

'Couldn't be surer. I remember when I first started dating, the one piece of advice my dad gave me. He said that it wasn't sleeping with someone that was the problem—the problem only arose when you woke up the next morning. So he told me always to stop and think, to ask myself if I'd feel embarrassed waking up beside this person.'

'And I take it Constantine passed Daddy's embarrassment test?'

'Absolutely. I didn't feel anything but happiness at waking up next to him. In fact it was quite the most wonderful feeling of my life. It couldn't have felt more right.'

'Then I couldn't be happier for you. When's the wedding?'

'Wedding? Oh, Ivan, don't rush things. We've only just got back together.'

'But he loved you enough to want you as his wife before. If you ask me, Constantine doesn't let grass grow under his feet. When he wants something, he goes for it, and nothing gets in his way. It's my bet that he'll have you hauled before a priest and a ring on your finger before you have time to say, "I do."'

'That would be wonderful.' In spite of her determination not to build up her hopes too quickly, Grace admitted to the dream she prayed would come true. 'Oh, Ivan, I hope so!'

'So do I, sweetie. Because you know I've always wanted to be there on the day you become Constantine's bride.'

Constantine's bride. Constantine's *bride*. Grace hugged the words to herself throughout the rest of the day.

Was it possible? Could it really be true that the whole nightmare was over and that she was really going to have a fairytale happy ending?

Certainly, from the way the day went, it seemed it might be so. Everything appeared to have been touched by the same magic that had brought her and Constantine together. Her work progressed effortlessly, a new campaign she had thought up for a particularly difficult and picky client won instant approval, and even the notoriously unreliable English spring weather decided to put on a show of mild sunshine and blue skies.

So it was with a light heart and a sense of breathless anticipation that she pushed open the door on her arrival home that evening.

The first thing she checked was her answer-machine. There was bound to be a message from Constantine. He would have had time in between his so important meetings. If she knew Constantine he would have *made* time, no matter how difficult it was.

But the glowing red letters on the machine obstinately recorded the number nought, and when she pressed the relevant button the mechanically flat tones of the recorded message informed her blankly that she had no messages.

No messages. For the first time that day a hint of doubt assailed her, sending an apprehensive shiver creeping over her skin.

I'll call you.

Constantine's voice sounded inside her head, but this time she subjected the words to a more intense scrutiny and analysis.

She had been so sure that he meant what he'd said. That he had every intention of phoning her just as soon as it was possible. But now a nasty, sneaking doubt made her frown uncertainly, white teeth worrying at the skin on her bottom lip.

I'll call you.

How many times had that phrase been used to cover up the fact that the speaker meant the exact opposite? Hadn't she and every other woman she knew been assured that someone would call, only to find, after long nights spent in waiting for the phone to ring, that they had had no interest at all in furthering the relationship? That in fact they were already seeing someone else?

No! She couldn't believe it! She *wouldn't* believe it! Constantine didn't make promises he couldn't keep, and if he gave his word, he stuck to it.

No, he must just have been every bit as busy as he had anticipated. He had been caught up in the problems he was here to sort out and hadn't been able to snatch a single minute to himself.

But he would ring. All she had to do was wait. She would get herself something to eat. Maybe even have a long, scented bath—with the phone handset carefully within reach, of course. She would linger in the warm water until she felt completely relaxed, then she would use the perfumed body lotion she had bought the previous week-end...

Hot colour suffused her skin at the thought of just why she was indulging in this way, the final end towards which all this luxuriating and pampering would lead when Constantine finally arrived. If she was lucky, he might not pause too long between 'Hello' and 'Let's go to bed', and that was just the way she wanted it.

But by the time she had carried out her carefully planned programme, dawdling over her meal, lingering in the bath until the water was almost cold, before pulling on a soft peach towelling robe, and still there was no sign of Constantine, her mood changed yet again.

'Oh, where *are* you?'

She spoke the words aloud, unable to keep them in any longer.

'What's happened to you? Surely you can't be still at work at this time?'

But of course he could, and often had been in the past. Constantine was the archetypal workaholic: totally absorbed in what he was doing, and prepared to devote all the hours in a day to it if that was what it took to achieve the result he wanted. As his fiancée, she had often complained about feeling neglected, that she'd resented the little time he could spare to devote to her at the end of his business commitments. And he had appeared repentant. He had promised to change once they were married.

Once they were married.

Grace took the mug of tea she had made into the sitting room and curled up in one of the armchairs, her feet tucked underneath her, her mood suddenly flat and reflective. They had never married. Paula's lies; the wicked, malicious stories she had made up had seen to that.

It had begun with a knock at the door.

From nowhere it seemed that the past had reached out

to enclose her. That it had taken her back to the time, exactly two years before, when her whole world had fallen apart.

She had spent the day at Constantine's apartment. The apartment that, in less than a week, was to have become her home too. It had been a Sunday night, and on the following Saturday she and Constantine were to have been married. This was to have been her last weekend as a single girl.

They had shared a long, intimate meal together, lingering over a bottle of wine, until at last, reluctantly, she had decided it was time to leave.

'Don't go,' Constantine murmured, one long hand toying softly with the strands of her hair. 'Stay tonight.'

'Constantine, you know I can't! You agreed to wait, and there's only another week to go. That's not so very long.'

'True,' Constantine conceded, getting reluctantly to his feet. 'But I have to admit that this old-fashioned idea of yours of insisting on holding out until the wedding night has made the waiting to make you mine even harder to bear.'

'But think how special that first night will be.'

Grace had to struggle not to show how his use of the phrase *holding out* had disturbed her. It made her actions sound almost perverse and selfish, not the carefully thought out beliefs they actually were.

'I have done nothing *but* think! If you only knew how I lie awake at night—alone in my bed...how I long to come to you...'

His footsteps silent on the thick pile of the rust-coloured carpet, he came towards her, black eyes fixed on her face.

'To take you in my arms...'

Suiting action to the words, he gathered her up, lifting her clean out of her seat.

'Kiss you here...and here...and here...'

Grace's breath caught in her throat as his warm mouth caressed her cheeks, her lips, her softly closed eyelids. Her senses swam, her blood firing immediately in frantic response to his caresses.

'Kiss you until you're senseless with wanting, aching with hunger as I am, until you're—'

'Constantine!' With an effort Grace forced herself to control the raging pulse that throbbed through her veins. 'No!'

With more force than was strictly necessary she pushed him away when he tried to kiss her again. It was either that or succumb to his sensual enticement right here and now. On this settee, or even the floor; she doubted if she'd have cared. Constantine wasn't the only one who had found her decree of celibacy difficult to live with.

Constantine drew in a deep, ragged breath, obviously fighting for control.

'You are a cruel woman, Grace Vernon,' he told her with mock severity. 'Cruel and hard, and a wicked tease.'

If only Constantine knew, Grace thought to herself. If only he realised just how difficult she found it to say no to him, then he would never think her hard, or cruel, for imposing such restrictions on him.

He might think her crazy, though. Because although he had tried to understand and appreciate her wish to hold back on the physical consummation of their relationship until their wedding night, he wasn't averse to applying a little pressure, just enough to test her resolve.

And there had been so many times that she had been tempted. After all, this was the man she loved, the man she wanted to marry. She wasn't exactly indifferent to him! Quite the opposite, in fact. He had only to smile at her and she melted inside, to touch her and her heart started to race, kiss her and she went up in flames. She wanted him so much it was like a constant nagging hunger. But she also wanted their first time together to be so very special.

She knew it was unusual, definitely unfashionable. But, having grown up watching her mother's casual attitude to sex and the ideal of faithfulness in a marriage, and the pain it had caused her father, she had always known she wanted something very different for herself. When she married, she had vowed, it would be for ever, and that for ever would begin with the very first time she had ever made love.

But she hadn't reckoned with the reality of the physical desire she felt for Constantine. When she had first met him she had been knocked completely off balance. He had left her feeling as if she had been picked up by a howling tornado, whirled high into the air and deposited somewhere that looked like the world she knew and yet was so very different from that comfortable place. Every light seemed brighter, every colour sharper, every sound intensified, and all her senses were on red alert, hypersensitively attuned to him.

Those thoughts were still in her mind when she reached her home, lingering in her head as she made herself a cup of coffee before going to bed. Her father and Diana were out, having dinner together, and Paula was away, staying with a friend. She was heading for the stairs when the knock came at the door.

'Who on earth...?'

The words shrivelled on her lips as she saw the identity of the late caller, and the state she was in.

'Paula! What are you doing here?'

Concern paled her face, shadowed her eyes, as she took in her stepsister's ragged breathing, her glittering eyes and the evidence of tears down her colourless cheeks.

'What is it? What's wrong?'

'Grace...' Her stepsister ran into Grace's arms with a choking sob and a cry of, 'Oh, Gracie, I'm so sorry!'

'Sorry?'

Grace could only frown her confusion, her heart jerking inside her chest in some intuitive premonition of horror, of something that was terribly wrong, but she couldn't even begin to guess what.

She had never seen her stepsister in such a state before. Normally Paula was full of the confidence of youth, bubbling over with self-assurance. At nineteen, almost twenty, she had the sort of dark-haired, blue-eyed voluptuous prettiness that had men buzzing round her like bees round a honeypot. But today those brilliant sapphire-coloured eyes were red-rimmed from weeping, her pale skin blotchy and marked.

'Paula, darling...' Grace smoothed a soothing hand over the long deep brown hair. 'What is it? Look, come and sit down and tell me everything.'

'I—I can't...' her stepsister managed unevenly. 'You—you'll hate me!'

'Hate you?' Had she heard right? 'What do you mean, Paula? I could never hate you. You're my sister.'

They had first met when she was fourteen, Paula just a schoolgirl of eleven. Grace had always longed not to be an only child, and she had taken the younger girl, lost and alone following her father's early death and her widowed mother's move to London, very much under her wing. Later, when Grace's father and Paula's mother had married, Grace had opened her heart to her new stepsister, and at first her affection had seemed to be reciprocated.

But just lately the younger girl had been mixing with a rather wild crowd from the office where she worked; she had become rebellious and defiant, and she regarded her older sister as dull, too conventional and altogether boring. As a result, the friendship had become rather strained, almost to breaking point. But Grace had always had a special place in her heart for Paula.

So, now, 'You can tell me anything,' she told her. 'Anything at all.'

'Even if it's about *him*? About Constantine.'

'What about Constantine?'

Paula caught hold of her sister's hands, clutching them so tightly that Grace winced in pain.

'Grace, darling, I'm so sorry about this—but I just couldn't live with myself if I didn't tell you. I can't let you delude yourself any longer.'

'Delude myself... About what?'

'About that pig of a man you're engaged to. You can't let things go any further. You can't marry him! He's totally promiscuous—hasn't got a faithful bone in his body!'

'No...' Grace shook her head firmly, refusing even to consider the idea. 'No, Paula. I don't know where you've got this idea from, but you have to be mistaken. Constantine would never...'

'Oh, wouldn't he? You say you don't know where I got this idea from, but I didn't *get it* from anyone. I didn't need to—I know all the facts I need from personal experience. Because, you see, the woman your fiancé was unfaithful with—one of the many, for all I know—was me. He slept with *me*.'

'*No!*'

It was a cry of pain, the sound of a heart breaking.

'*Yes,*' Paula insisted. 'Yes! Yes! Yes! He's been after me for weeks—pushing, pushing, pushing! I told him I wasn't interested—that you were my sister—but he just laughed...'

Grace's shadowed gaze was concentrated on Paula, seeing the distress in her eyes, the way her hands clenched and unclenched nervously.

'I tried to resist him, Grace, I really did! But then that weekend in February, when you were away seeing your mother, everything came to a head. I was alone in the house and he turned up. I thought he'd come to see you, but he said—he said that of course he knew you weren't there, that while the cat was away the mice could play.'

Paula drew a long, shuddering breath and straightened her shoulders.

'He'd brought a bottle of wine, and he asked me to share it with him.'

'He got you drunk?' Grace couldn't conceal her horror.

'Not exactly—just a bit tiddly. But then he started coming on to me again. He was insistent, forceful. I said no; he said yes. I retreated; he followed. And then he caught hold of me and kissed me. He—he said that he knew it was what I really wanted, that I was only playing hard to get. That all he did was think about me when he was alone in his bed. He told me that I was a wicked tease—a cruel, hard woman…'

All he did was think…a wicked tease…a cruel, hard woman. The words reverberated inside Grace's skull, making her head reel as if from actual physical blows.

Less than an hour before, Constantine had used those exact words to her when he had tried to seduce her, to entice her into making love with him. And now to hear them repeated, quoted as they had been used to another woman…! Were they, then, the lines of a practised seducer, a man who churned out exactly the same lines for each new conquest? The thought was like bitter acid inside her, eating away at her heart.

'And he said he was frustrated as hell. That the other women in his life hadn't kept him dangling like this. That your insistence on holding out until the wedding was more than he could take. He wanted a real woman, someone who knew her own mind, not a—'

'That's enough!' Grace couldn't bear to hear any more.

'Oh, Grace, I'm sorry! I wish I hadn't had to tell you this! But please believe what I've said—for your own sake.

If he's done it once, he'll do it again—probably has, for all I know. Grace—think about it!'

Think about it! She couldn't do anything else! She knew she couldn't go to bed now. She couldn't rest, couldn't sleep, couldn't do anything until she had confronted Constantine.

And the terrible thing was that all the way to Constantine's apartment she could see how it might have been. She knew so well the cold force of her fiancé's single-minded determination, the steel-hard ruthlessness that drove him. When he was set on something, he could sweep aside anything he considered irrelevant, trampling any foolish, feeble objections under the soles of his highly polished handmade shoes.

So had that merciless power been turned on Paula? And if it had been combined with the potent sexuality, the devastatingly carnal appeal that Constantine also possessed, the seductive eloquence of his silken tongue, then what woman could have resisted?

Paula was so much younger. Fresh out of school and naively impressionable—though she'd be the first to deny that description—she was no match for a sophisticated, experienced man of the world like Constantine.

Hadn't Grace herself been tempted so often by his huskily whispered enticements, their sensual appeal heightened by his beautifully accented deep voice, until she had come close to succumbing, to abandoning her long-held and deeply felt principles?

'How could you?' The words burst from her as soon as she was through the door. 'How could you do this to me? How could you even believe that you'd get away with it? That I wouldn't find out and...'

'Hold on a minute.' Constantine's tone was almost as harsh as her own. 'Precisely what is it I'm supposed to have done?'

'Oh, don't give me that! You know—Paula has told me everything...'

She had to force the dreadful story out, finding it unbearable even to tell it, hating the way the words felt on her tongue.

'It's a lie.'

It was too quick, too pat. Feeling raw and distraught, her heart just an anguished, burning pain, as if someone was pulling it to pieces bit by bit, she needed more. So much more.

'That's it? "It's a lie" and I'm supposed to believe you?'

'Grace, nothing happened. This is all some crazy story that Paula's made up.'

'And why would she do that?'

'She has some fantasy—'

'Fantasy!' Grace couldn't believe what she was hearing. 'This wasn't any sort of fantasy! You didn't see her! You didn't see the state she was in!'

'No, I didn't, but it wouldn't change anything. She lied.'

'And why would she lie about something like this? She's my sister! And besides, some of it she didn't have to tell me—some of it I already knew. Like the fact that there have been other women in your life. Sophisticated women with no hang-ups about the physical side of a relationship. And are you going to deny the fact that you've been finding it hard to wait for our wedding night?'

Constantine raked both his hands through the darkness of his hair, his expression grim as he shook his head.

'I'd be the liar if I did!'

'And you've always admitted to a weakness for petite, curvy women with black hair and blue eyes.'

'So now I'm tried and condemned because of some innocent remark I made months ago?' Constantine's tone had changed noticeably, and something dangerous sparked in his eyes. 'If you're not prepared to believe me, is there any point in continuing this conversation?'

'I need the truth! Did you do this?'

Constantine's arrogant dark head lifted even higher, nostrils flared, jet-black eyes blazing.

'I have already answered that question. Can you have any doubt—?'

'Quite frankly, I have nothing *but* doubts!' Grace flung at him. 'And, feeling like this, there is no way I can go ahead with our marriage!'

'You're cancelling the wedding? Over *this*!'

He made it sound as if it was the proverbial storm in a teacup. This wasn't what she had expected. She had thought—had hoped—that he would take her in his arms and tell her that he adored her, that he worshipped the ground she walked on, and he would rather die than let anything hurt her.

'Postponing it, certainly. I need time to think.'

'No, you don't.'

'I *do*! Constantine, you have to—'

'Have to!' Constantine repeated on a note of pure scorn. 'You're on quite the wrong track, my sweet Grace, if you think I'm obliged to do anything at all! I've said all I'm going to say. The ball is in your court, and nowhere else, my darling. It's your move.'

Her move! Grace couldn't even think what the words meant, never mind do anything about them.

'Constantine...'

And then it happened. Just as she looked into the hard, set mask that was his face, just as ebony eyes met grey, locking and...

The room spun sickeningly round her. Grace had to put out a hand to clutch at the nearest chair for support. It couldn't be! Dear God, please let it not be true!

Because impossibly, unbelievably, suddenly Constantine's

gaze was not quite steady. It was his stare that wavered, just for a second. And that second was enough to reveal another, very different expression that had lain hidden until now. Underneath the confident pride, the arrogant self-assurance, lurked something she could only describe as fear and…and…

And *guilt*, her unwilling mind supplied, her heart stopping dead in horror.

A moment later he blinked and it was gone. But she had seen it, and it was enough to shatter her belief that he could still convince her all was well and she would fall into his arms on a wave of heady relief.

'I want to go home,' she said drearily, all life, all feeling stripped from her voice so that it was as flat and dead as her thoughts.

And the truly frightening thing was that Constantine didn't argue. She had been nerving herself for a fight, struggling to dredge up enough emotional strength to resist him, only to find it wasn't needed. Instead, he turned without a word, reaching for the telephone.

'I'll ring for a taxi,' he said, not a flicker of regret or any other reaction showing on his face. 'I'd offer to drive you, but I very much doubt that either of us would want to be alone with the other any longer tonight.'

But it didn't end there. Because eventually Paula admitted that she had lied. Somehow Grace's father managed to work on her stepsister's conscience until at last Paula owned up to the terrible jealousy she had always felt for Grace.

'You were always so damn perfect! So tall and slim and blonde—and a real male-magnet! No man ever gave me a second look when you came into the room. And if I brought a boyfriend home, he was guaranteed to lose interest the minute he set eyes on you. It was always, "Is *she* your sister? You're not at all alike, are you?'' until I was ready to scream.'

'But, Paula, that wasn't my fault.' Grace was shocked to realise the thoughts that Paula had been harbouring all this time, the resentment she had let grow into something more dangerous. 'I didn't know it was happening.'

'Oh, sure you didn't!' her stepsister scorned. 'Little Miss Perfect just didn't realise that she was flirting with every man I've ever liked! Well, I knew—and I didn't like it. And I vowed that I'd get even. That one day I'd steal a man from you as you did from me.'

And the man she'd set her sights on was Constantine. Waiting and watching, letting her jealousy fester deep inside, she had finally made her move just at the point where it would have the most deadly effect.

But somehow Grace couldn't bring herself to care about Paula's behaviour. Her heart was soaring, excitement bubbling up inside her. She couldn't wait until she could speak to Constantine again and tell him that his name had been cleared. That with Paula's confession there was nothing now to stand in the way of their wedding. She loved him, and she couldn't wait to be his bride. They could be married within the month.

But Constantine didn't react in the way she had expected at all.

CHAPTER FIVE

A SOUND from the street brought Grace suddenly wide awake, throwing off the world of the past and its unhappy memories. A car door slamming and hurried footsteps coming towards the house.

In a rush she got to her feet and dashed to the window, pulling back the curtains so that she could see out.

Constantine, his strong figure outlined by the street lamps, a huge bouquet in one hand. He was obviously as impatient to see her as she was to see him and he mounted the steps to the door two at a time, reaching the top before she really had time to register he was truly there.

Delight put wings on her feet as she raced to let him in. So what if he was late? He was here, and that was all that mattered.

'At last!'

She couldn't hold back the exclamation as she flung open the door, her heart doing a tap dance of joy inside her chest as her eyes feasted on the wonderful sight of him. With his tall frame sheathed in a superbly tailored suit in charcoal-grey, immaculate white shirt and discreet burgundy tie, he was no longer the trainee waiter he had claimed to be last night, but every inch the city man. Constantine Kiriazis of the Kiriazis Corporation. The man who had companies like the agency she worked in for breakfast.

'I'd just about given up on you.'

Not the most auspicious of beginnings, she realised as she saw the swift frown that drew his black brows together. She had meant to imply that she had been impatient to see him, but had only succeeded in making it sound like a reproof.

'It is—what…?'

A swift glance at the clock stunned her. Perhaps she had meant to reproach him after all.

'It's ten-thirty, Constantine! I was starting to think about going to bed.'

'So I see.'

Brilliant black eyes seared over her body in the cosy but hardly glamorous towelling robe.

'That's fine by me,' he drawled insolently.

'Fine…'

Grace found she was actually struggling to speak. The audacity of the man! Okay, she was glad to see him, but that didn't mean he could turn up as he liked, when he liked, and expect her to fall straight into bed with him.

'You could have phoned. I don't like to feel taken for granted.'

'Grace, I have been working,' Constantine explained with an exaggerated patience that expressed more of the annoyance he was trying to keep in check than any true equanimity.

'All this time?'

'I had dinner with a client. That ended…' He consulted his watch briefly. 'Half an hour ago. It took some time to get over to this side of London, and I had to make a minor detour on the way. And as for feeling taken for granted, perhaps this will help.'

The bouquet he held out would have taken anyone's breath away. Lilies had always been Grace's favourite flowers; not that she ever had enough spare cash to indulge herself. So to be presented with this profusion of the glorious blooms—three dozen at the very least—was absolutely overwhelming.

'Oh, Constantine, thank you! They're beautiful—gorgeous!'

And what mattered most was that he had found time in the middle of what had obviously been a very busy day to think of her and arrange to have the bouquet made up. Okay, so men like Constantine didn't do the ordering and suchlike themselves; they had teams of minions to perform such tasks for them. But he must have specified exactly what type of flowers he wanted. Which meant he remembered her personal likes and dislikes.

'But I wasn't really cross. Honestly, you didn't need to...'

'I usually give my women flowers. Particularly on a first date.'

Grace was suddenly thankful for the way that her head was bent to the flowers, the fall of her hair concealing her momentary reaction, the flicker of pain across her face that she couldn't quite suppress.

'Your women,' she echoed when she felt she could manage to sound as if it didn't matter. 'I hope I'm more to you than that.'

His unexpected silence brought her head up in a rush, just in time to catch the expression on his face. With the memory of the freezing lack of emotion he had displayed when she had cancelled their wedding still vivid in her mind, she found the similarity between the two made her blood run cold.

But then, as swiftly as it had appeared, the look was gone. In its place was a glance of sexually devastating significance slanted at her from gleaming eyes.

'Right now, you're everything I want,' he told her huskily. 'Grace, for God's sake, come here and say hello properly.'

It was like a salve to the smart of uncertainty she had

felt. Willingly she went into his arms, holding her face up for his kiss.

His lips were still cold from the night air outside, but the heat of his passion soon erased any lingering chill. As his mouth crushed hers in urgent demand she felt her own blood heating in response, her own lips parting under his, allowing the practised invasion of his tongue.

'You smell delicious,' Constantine eventually murmured against her hair. 'And you feel wonderful. But *this*...' arrogant hands plucked contemptuously at the peach towelling robe '...is hardly the most flattering of garments.'

'It's the only one I've got. Remember, I never even expected that I would be entertaining you tonight.'

'I shall buy you a better one. What would you prefer—silk—satin?'

'Constantine, you don't need to buy me presents.'

'No?'

A dark eyebrow winged upwards in exaggerated surprise.

'I thought all women liked gifts—the more expensive the better.'

There was an edge to his voice that made Grace frown uneasily, reminding her of the almost dismissive *my women* he had used earlier.

'Oh, I like them... Which reminds me—I'd better put these flowers in water before they start to wilt. I just hope I have enough vases. Constantine, you've been hopelessly extravagant.'

Constantine's shrug as he followed her into the kitchen was a wordless reminder that a bunch of flowers, however large and lavish, was hardly going to make even the slightest dent in his personal fortune.

'I thought they would please you.'

'Oh, they do!'

Suddenly and inexplicably she felt anxious and uneasy. Inside the confined space of her small kitchen,

Constantine's lean, powerful frame seemed impossibly big and strong, totally dominating the room. She felt as if every cell, every nerve-ending was sharply attuned to the potent sexual magnetism of the man behind her. So much so that her skin heated under the robe, all the tiny hairs on the back of her neck lifting in instinctive response at the sound of his breathing, the tiniest movement.

'Oh, this is ridiculous!' she muttered to herself.

'What is ridiculous?'

To her consternation Constantine's sharp hearing had caught the mumbled comment, his soft question making her jump so that the water in the vase she was filling went everywhere.

'I haven't offered you anything to…to drink,' she amended hastily.

Anything to eat she had been about to say, only recalling just in time that he had been at dinner with a client only an hour before.

'Would you like coffee? Wine?'

'Oh, Grace…'

Constantine's laughter was unexpected, bringing her whirling round to study his face in order to try and understand the reason for it. Her heart lurched sharply in uncontrollable response to the sudden softening of the strongly carved features, the new warmth in his eyes.

'Grace, *pethi mou*, I believe we played out exactly this scene last night. And my response now is precisely the same as it was then.'

'You don't want anything to drink?'

'No.'

'And you're not hungry?'

'No—not for food anyway.'

He didn't need to elaborate. It was there in his eyes, in the sensual curve of his mouth. He had said he wasn't hungry, but there was no denying the raw need that was stamped on to his strong-boned features, drawing the skin tight over the broad cheekbones.

As she watched, her mouth drying painfully, she saw the warmth fade from his eyes to be replaced by another, very different form of heat. A blazing, scorching fire that made her feel as if she was in the path of a laser beam, one that had the power to strip a layer of skin from her body, leaving her deeply vulnerable and exposed.

'Grace,' he said on a very different note from before. 'Come here.'

Without quite being aware that she had moved, she was suddenly in his arms, being held close against the hard lines of his body, hearing the heavy beat of his heart against the strong wall of his chest.

'Grace, my sweet, beautiful Grace, there is one reason and one reason alone that I came here tonight. And that was not for food, or wine, or anything but this...'

The gentle sensuality of his kiss took her breath away, making her head spin. It soothed all the ragged feelings of moments before, driving every nervous thought, every uncertainty from her mind. He was here for her and for no other reason, and that was what made her heart sing.

She'd been thinking about the past; that was the problem. Remembering how it had once been. And those memories had coloured her thoughts, darkening them and making her irrationally fearful. She had to put that past behind her, far, far behind, and move forward into the bright new future that had dawned so unexpectedly.

'Constantine...' His name was just a sigh on her lips, a sound of pure pleasure blending into a longing that he heard, and laughed at in soft triumph.

'I know, sweetheart, I know. I feel exactly that way too. Today has felt like a lifetime. I couldn't work, couldn't concentrate. All I could think of was getting through the hours and getting back here so that I could kiss you...'

He suited action to the words, his former gentleness changing swiftly, moving into a hungry demand that had Grace responding with eager enthusiasm.

'So that I could touch you...' Constantine managed, his voice thickening noticeably when at last, reluctantly, they had to break apart to draw in a much needed breath.

It was only when his hands slid underneath the cotton towelling that Grace realised he had tugged at the tie belt that held her robe closed, letting it fall open, revealing the simple white nightdress she wore underneath.

'Now this is better,' he murmured, pushing the towelling robe down from her shoulders and pressing his mouth to the smooth flesh exposed by the narrow shoestring straps. 'Much better...'

'Constantine!' Grace gasped as firm white teeth closed around one strap, tugging it gently until it slid over her left shoulder and hung loose over her arm.

With her hands and forearms imprisoned by the confining folds of her robe she could only stand immobile as that tormenting mouth inched its way across her shoulder and back towards her throat. Making a momentary detour along the fine lines of her neck, Constantine marked out a trail of burning kisses along her collarbone and across to the other side. The right-hand strap went the same way as the left, the loosened top of her nightdress sliding downwards to reveal the smooth slopes of her upper breasts.

His lips followed its path, his hot tongue occasionally flicking out to taste the creamy flesh he had exposed. The sizzling pleasure of his caresses made Grace shift restlessly, arching her neck, her head flung back in delight, an uncontrolled moan escaping her.

A moment later she was catching her breath in her throat as that proud dark head moved even lower, to the tightness of her breasts where her nipples thrust against the soft cotton of her nightdress. First on one side and then the other he took the throbbing peaks into the heat of his mouth through the fine material, moistening each with his tongue before he sucked hard. Stinging pleasure radiated from that one, devastating focus point, and arrowed with white-hot force straight to the point between her thighs where her hunger centred, pulsing fiercely.

At the same time, hard, warm hands were sliding under the hem of the short nightdress, pushing it upwards, higher and higher. Bronzed fingers slid over the slender length of her thigh, over the curve of her hips, and then angled down to the most intimate spot of all, sliding deep inside her, stroking rhythmically.

'*Constantine!*'

Grace shuddered wildly, thrusting herself against him, hungry, demanding. The need she felt was too intense, the delight too close to pain for her to say any more. She could only whimper in ecstatic response, her hands clutching at his shoulders, supporting herself with difficulty.

'Steady, sweetheart...' Constantine's voice was raw and husky, as if it came from a painfully tight throat. 'Easy now...'

Easy! She didn't want to take things easy! The only thing that would *ease* the way she felt was the feel of his possession, of his hard, strong body blending with her own. She wanted him to take her, take them both to that devastating, brilliant place where the world and everyone in it ceased to be and there was only the two of them and the blazing consummation they created between them.

But already Constantine was moving his hands away, depriving her of the caresses that had so excited her. His mouth moved up the fine lines of her throat, kissed her mouth briefly as he smoothed down her nightdress with almost matter-of-fact control.

'Constantine...' The name broke in the middle, her voice ragged, uneven, pleading. 'Constantine, please....'

His laughter was soft against her hair.

'Grace, honey, be realistic. There isn't enough room in this kitchen for two consenting mice, let alone a couple of fully-grown adults. I think we'd better continue this somewhere more comfortable.'

The idea of continuing reassured her. And so when he held out his hand she put hers into it willingly, following him like a sleepwalker.

He led her not, as she had expected, to the bedroom, but to the darkened living room, where the only light came from the fire in the grate, now burning low, the coals glowing red-hot. Standing before it, he eased the cotton robe from her body, arranging it on the floor at their feet.

Gently he laid her down on the makeshift rug, pausing only to strip away his own clothes before he came down beside her.

'This will have to go,' he muttered, taking the white nightdress in two strong hands.

With one powerful movement he ripped it in two and tossed it aside, exposing the pale flesh underneath, the soft curves coloured by the glow of the fire.

'So, now, where were we?'

Like the fire, Grace's desperately aroused body had not actually cooled, but only quietened. And just as the fire would have needed only a moment's attention before it once more burst into flames, so she too only needed the slightest touch of his hands and lips to be once again at fever-pitch.

Within a couple of heated seconds she was reaching for Constantine, pulling him over her, even sliding her hands between them, closing over the slick, hot hardness of him, guiding him into her in her urgency to know his possession.

Holding him tight, with her arms clamped around his narrow waist, her legs tangled with his, she abandoned all restraint. Lifting her hips in the sure, instinctive rhythm that she knew would pleasure them both, she took control, driving him onward with every move, every touch. Above her, she felt his muscles tighten, heard his muttered curse as he abandoned himself to her lead, taking the secondary role for once.

A bubble of triumphant laughter burst from her as the pace mounted higher and higher. With her own body burning in electric sensation, she was supremely aware of his, and the response she was drawing from it. Constantine Kiriazis, the man who was always in control, always the epitome of restraint, was lost, adrift on a sea of sensuality, and it was all because of her. It was more than she had ever dreamed of, and she couldn't hold back a wild cry of ecstasy as with one final thrust she took him with her into the blazing consummation they were striving for.

The scene that Grace woke to on the following morning was almost a carbon copy of the previous day, except for one thing. This time Constantine was already dressed when she finally forced her heavy lids open, and he was leaning over the bed, placing a small gift-wrapped parcel on the side-table.

'What are you doing?'

'Going to work.' As before, it was short to the point of rudeness.

'But...'

There was something wrong with that, if only she could get her head round it. Once again, it had been hours before they had slept, and exhaustion was catching up on her.

'But it's Saturday!' she pronounced at last on a note of triumph at having forced herself to think.

'I have a lot to do. I am here to work...'

'Not at the weekend! Oh, Constantine, please...' she pleaded. 'No one gets up this early!'

'At home, I rise early all the time,' he contradicted her.

'That way I can get more done before the day really heats up.'

'In Greece, perhaps, but I really doubt that it's going to get too hot to work in April in London. Constantine, I had plans for today...'

'And so do I,' he returned shortly, running a hand over his hair to smooth it.

She could still remember how it had been to feel that jet-black silk under her touch, Grace thought hungrily. In the height of passion she had clutched at it, fingers twisting, tugging, until she was sure it must have hurt. But never once had Constantine complained.

Instead he had actively encouraged her.

'Grace, *pethi mou*,' he had whispered in the darkness of the night, his accent sounding so much stronger to ears made sensitive because she couldn't see. 'I wouldn't know you for the same woman. I never guessed it could be like this—that you could be so exciting, so passionate...'

And she had wanted to turn to him and tell him that her response shouldn't surprise him. Didn't they say that absence made the heart grow fonder? Two years before, she would never have believed that she could have loved him any more than she did then. But, having spent two long, lonely years believing that she had lost him and that she would never see him again, she now knew the truth. And that truth was that what she had felt for him then had been like the tiny, flickering flame of a candle compared to the wild, blazing fire that was her love now.

But even as she opened her mouth to speak Constantine had blocked off her words with an urgent, demanding kiss. The hunger that she had thought was satiated proved instead to have simply been temporarily appeased, dampened down, not obliterated. Within the space of a couple of heartbeats she had been in the grip of it once again, words becoming totally superfluous as she'd found other, more satisfying ways to declare her love.

'But your plans won't be as much fun as mine.'

Deliberately she stretched lazily, letting the quilt that covered her slide provocatively low, exposing a large amount of creamy flesh, flushed pink from the warmth of the bed. A heady rush of very female triumph mixed with a hot flood of sensual awareness as she saw his brilliant black gaze drop to follow the slight movement, the convulsive swallow he could not control.

'I thought we'd wake up more slowly than this…'

A sensual little wriggle of her hips made it plain exactly how she had hoped to be woken.

'That we'd breakfast together…having showered together first, of course. Which might just mean that breakfast would turn into brunch.'

He was tempted, she knew. Just his silence told her that. The fact that Constantine, confident, assured Constantine, who was never at a loss for words, could find nothing to say told her that her suggestions had hit home.

But not hard enough. And Constantine wasn't as tempted as she had hoped. Because the next moment he had shaken his dark head resolutely, destroying her hopes in a second.

'No,' he declared, coolly inflexible. 'Not today.'

Grace's full mouth formed a soft moue of protest and disappointment.

'Then when?'

'When the time is suitable. Grace…'

Her name sounded an ominous warning note as she tried to speak again.

'You must learn not to make demands. I will be here when it is possible. But I cannot dally with you all day long. My work is important.'

'I think I got that message,' Grace muttered petulantly.

I cannot dally with you... I will be here when it is possible. When he could fit her in, it sounded like.

'But I also think I deserve better than that.'

'And why is that, *pethi mou*?'

It was low and dangerous, fiendishly soft. But Grace was past heeding.

'You can't just come round here when it suits you, stay for just as long as it suits you...'

Constantine's sigh was a perfect blend of resignation and irritation, something in the sound flooding her with apprehension.

'I left you a gift.'

'What?'

It was such an unexpected change of tack that it threw her completely. She could only blink in confusion as Constantine reached for the parcel he had placed on the bedside table and held it out to her.

'I thought you would find it when you woke.'

There was something wrong here, Grace thought uneasily. Every instinct she possessed screamed at her that things were not as she'd thought, not as she wanted. And yet there was nothing concrete on which she could pin her feelings, no grounds for the suspicion that buzzed along her nerves like uncomfortable pins and needles.

'Look,' Constantine continued with careful patience when she could only stare at the gold-wrapped gift box he held, unable to find the strength to bring herself to reach out for it, 'I'll stay while you open it...'

The carved mouth curled slightly at the corners.

'Then you will be able to thank me properly.'

Her movements as stiff and jerky as some wind-up automaton, Grace held out a hand and he let the little box fall into it.

Slowly, carefully, almost as if she feared she might find some deadly snake or spider underneath the pretty paper,

Grace peeled away the wrapping, eased off the lid and finally lifted the cotton wool padding that protected the contents.

'Oh…'

It was all she could manage. Her mind seemed to have blown a fuse.

She knew what her reaction *should* be. She should make some sound of delight. Say, Oh, Constantine, it's beautiful! just as she had said about the flowers last night. And he obviously expected that she would fling her arms around him, rain kisses on the lean, hard planes of his cheeks. That she should *thank him properly*.

Which she would have done normally.

Because the delicate gold bangle that the box contained *was* beautiful. And under normal circumstances she would have been happy to receive it, delighted by such a generous present.

So what was it that changed this moment from normal circumstances into something that froze her tongue and kept her eyes fixed on the opened parcel, unable to look into Constantine's face for fear of what she might see there?

'It—it's very nice,' she managed shakily.

'Nice!' Constantine exploded. '*Theos*, Grace, *nice* is for chocolates, a card, or a pen, perhaps. What is wrong? I thought all women liked jewellery.'

And that was when the truth dawned on her. When she realised just why this situation was ringing warning bells loud and clear in her mind.

I thought all women liked gifts—the more expensive the better. From her memories of the previous night, his words came back to haunt her.

I usually give my women flowers. That was what he had said as he'd handed over the ridiculously extravagant bouquet of flowers.

My women…. All women.

Her head came up sharply, tossing her blonde hair back.

'But I'm not just one of "all women"!' she declared angrily, grey eyes flashing defiance. 'I think I'm rather more than that!'

He didn't move, didn't say a word, but she suddenly knew that she was on very dangerous ground indeed. It was there in the tightening of the muscles in his jaw, the cold, obsidian stare, his very stillness.

'And what, precisely, gives you that impression?' he asked, each word seeming to be formed in letters of ice, so that Grace shivered violently, as if they had actually landed cruelly on her exposed skin.

'Well, I—I'm more than just any woman...'

Nervously she glanced at him, expecting some response. But Constantine didn't even blink, his eyes opaque, revealing nothing.

'I mean—I'm...'

That dangerous stillness was beginning to affect her ability to speak. It reminded her of nothing so much as the unmoving crouch of a savage hunting cat, waiting, watching, judging the precise moment at which to pounce. Her already taut nerves tightened even more, as if in anticipation of the brutal claws, the cruel teeth.

'Surely when we are married you won't...'

That got a response.

With a sudden, unexpected movement, Constantine uncoiled lithely from his place on the bed and got to his feet to stand towering over her, black eyes blazing a terrible rejection of her words.

'"When we are married",' he echoed, giving each word a freezingly precise enunciation. 'And what, my sweet Grace, makes you think that that prospect is on the cards?'

There was a sound inside Grace's skull like the buzzing of a thousand frantic, angry bees and her eyes blurred so that she could no longer see Constantine's dark face. Her head swam sickeningly and she fell back against the pillows, painfully aware of the fact that if she had been standing her legs would no longer have supported her. She felt as if all the blood had been drained from her body, leaving her limp as a puppet with all its strings cut.

'But I thought...'

Her voice failed her, croaking embarrassingly, and she had to swallow hard in order to be able to speak. And all the time Constantine just stood there, his cruel glare burning into her skin so that she feared she might actually be scarred where it touched.

'I mean—we—we were going to be married before, so naturally when we got back together again, I assumed...'

'You assumed wrong.' Brutally sharp, it slashed into her stumbling explanation with the force of a steel blade. 'Nothing was further from my mind.'

'Wrong?'

He couldn't have said that. She couldn't be hearing right! Somehow they'd got their wires crossed and she'd become confused. She hadn't really taken in what he'd said.

Drawing a deep, fortifying breath, she sat upright, straightening her shoulders. It was time she got this sorted out.

'Don't mess me about, Constantine, this is too important for that. You know what I mean. We were engaged before. You loved me and I loved you, so it's natural that we'll want to take up where we left off. Since you came back to me, it's obvious that you still want to marry me.'

Her words fell into a silence so deep and profound that she could almost feel it drawing in around her, closing her throat so that she found it impossible to breathe naturally. Her heart was beating frantically inside her chest, making the blood pound against her temples with a sound like distant thunder.

'It is not obvious to me at all,' Constantine said at last.

'Nothing in what you have said has any bearing on this matter at all. I'm afraid you have been totally deluded in your assessment of the situation.'

His tone took that *I'm afraid* to a point light-years away from any real concern.

'But just to ensure that there is no misunderstanding between us, let me make myself perfectly clear. I came back to you because I wanted you. Nothing more. Once I had seen you again, I found it physically impossible to live without making you mine. That is the sum total of my feelings, and anything else you have come up with is pure conjecture—the product of your over-active imagination. And one final point…'

When he paused, obviously to emphasise the importance of what he was about to say, Grace had to bite down hard on her lower lip in order to hold back a desperate, fearful cry of, Don't!

She had to fight a nasty, painful struggle with herself in order not to give in to her impulse to lift her hands and press them over her ears, blotting out the words that she sensed intuitively were going to taken her new-found happiness and destroy it as effectively and callously as Constantine had when he'd rejected her two years before. She didn't want to hear him speak, and yet she didn't have the strength to even try and stop him.

'If you have any foolish ideas in that pretty head of yours—dreams of weddings and rings and happy ever after—then I strongly recommend that you forget them. We tried that one, remember. It didn't work out. But whatever else may happen between us, there is one thing I am sure of, and that is that you will never be my wife.'

CHAPTER SIX

You will never be my wife.

The words were like a knife in her heart.

She had been so sure, so happy. She had thought...

No. Admit the truth. She had never actually stopped to *think*. She had just reacted on instinct, on emotion, and hadn't stopped to consider whether what she was doing was actually wise. And she certainly had never even considered that Constantine might have any motivation other than the love she had naively attributed to him.

Well, now she knew. And although what she really wanted to do was to scream, to let out her pain in a tirade of abuse, a strong sense of self-preservation made her impose a ruthless control over her face and voice in order to hide what she was feeling.

'Might I ask your reasons for that statement?'

The look Constantine turned on her was icily contemptuous, scathing in disbelief that she even had to ask the question.

'You know my reasons. Nothing at all has changed in the past two years. My opinion of you is no different now from what it was when you came crawling back to me the last time.'

'Crawling...!'

Oh, this was better! With the help of a much needed rush of anger at the scornfully insulting words he had tossed at her, Grace was able to straighten her back, lift her fair head proudly, and meet those cold black eyes head-on.

'I did not *crawl*! As I recall, I came to apologise. I had made a genuine mistake, and I wanted to put things right.'

'A mistake!'

The bitter cynicism with which he flung the word at her had the burn of acid on her soul.

'I doubt if you really know what the real "mistake" you made actually was!'

'Of course I know!'

Indignation brought Grace fully upright to glare at him furiously. But she regretted the impetuous movement as soon as she saw Constantine's appraising gaze drop to survey her naked torso, exposed by the way the quilt fell back to around her waist.

'Cover yourself up,' he commanded harshly.

For one wonderful, mindless second, Grace was sorely tempted to defy him. She even considered letting the covers fall even lower and flaunting her nudity just to show how little his presence affected him. But no sooner had the thought formed than it shrivelled again, all her confidence leaching away in the face of that baleful, cold-eyed stare.

But what finally destroyed her self-assurance completely was Constantine's voice. It was as cool and analytical as a knife, leaving her in no doubt that if she had hoped to incite a sexual response in the man before her, and so reduce his ability to think clearly, she had failed miserably. He was as unmoved by her appearance as he would have been by a dead salmon on a fishmonger's slab.

'I said, cover yourself up. You look ridiculous sitting there like that.'

'I would if I could!'

Grace struggled against the temptation to clutch the quilt up close to her. She had never felt so defenceless, so vulnerable, so thoroughly exposed, but she was damned if she was going to let him see that.

'But, if you recall, my robe is still in the other room.'

The thought of exactly why it was still in the living room, the memory of their impassioned lovemaking before the fire, almost destroyed her. She had to swallow hard to force down the sudden thickness in her throat. Refusing to let the hot tears that stung at her eyes even have a chance of falling, she forced herself to go on.

'And I'm sure that if I got out of bed in order to go and fetch it, you would find some other, even more insulting description of my behaviour—accuse me of parading my nakedness in front of you like a...'

'*Christos!*' Constantine muttered furiously, but she was relieved to see that he turned on his heel and marched out of the room, returning only seconds later with the peach towelling robe dangling from one finger.

In a gesture of haughty disdain he tossed it on to the bed beside her, discarding it swiftly, as if he felt that to touch it any longer might contaminate him.

'Put it on!' he commanded arrogantly. 'Then perhaps we might be able to continue this discussion rationally.'

'You weren't so quick to cover me up last night,' Grace retorted, struggling to pull on the robe without revealing any more of her naked body that she absolutely had to.

Even though it was crazy after all that had happened between them on the past two nights, she still wanted to scream at him to turn his back, give her some privacy. But she knew what his reply would be. That there wasn't a single inch of her body that he hadn't seen, caressed, and more during their lovemaking.

But then last night, and the night before, he hadn't made her feel so ashamed, so humiliated. Then he had treated her body as something beautiful, something to be revered and cherished. Now he was looking at her as if she was something particularly sordid and unpleasant that he had found dumped in the dustbin.

'Then you were only too keen to take my robe *off* me and keep it off.'

'Last night was last night. I had other things on my mind then. Are you ready to talk now?'

What she really wanted was to tell him to go to hell and never come back, but instead she contented herself with getting out of bed and drawing herself up to her full five foot ten, knotting the tie belt of her robe extra firmly round her slim waist as she did so.

'If we have to talk, then, yes. I suppose so. But if you don't mind I would prefer to continue this conversation in another room.' And if he did mind, she couldn't care less. 'It really doesn't seem at all suitable for a bedroom.'
With her head held high she marched past him out of the bedroom and into the sitting room, leaving him with no option but to follow.

'Now,' she began, turning to face him. 'I believe you were about to tell me just what sort of a mistake I made—in your opinion—two years ago.'

'Love requires absolute trust,' he pronounced inexorably, severe as a magistrate pronouncing judgement. 'As I told you at the time. When your trust was challenged you broke immediately. You actually believed I had done those appalling things. You had no faith in—'

'Constantine...'

Unable to bear the distance between them any longer, Grace moved forward, reaching out to take hold of his hands. With her shadowed grey eyes fixed on his face, she gripped his fingers firmly, as if by doing so she could will him to believe her.

'Paula was my *sister*!'

'And I was your *fiancé*!' Constantine flung at her, snatching away his hands as if her touch had actually burned him.

Swinging away from her, he strode to the other side of the room to stand, staring out of the window at the street, still silent and unoccupied at this early hour of the weekend. The tension in his back and shoulders, the way his hands were pushed deep into the pockets of his trousers told their own story of the struggle he was having to bring his black temper back under control.

At last he turned back again, and Grace quailed inwardly at what she saw in his face. Anger and contempt etched white lines around his nose and mouth, marking him outwardly with the feelings that burned deep inside.

'You couldn't trust me completely then, and I cannot trust you now. And that is why you will never be my wife.'

Well, she'd asked for it, Grace told herself unhappily. She'd insisted that he told her, and he had done just that, coldly and concisely.

She'd admitted that she'd been partly to blame, but Constantine's insistence on seeing everything in black and white—that she should have believed him, and only him— was every bit as uncompromising now as it had been then. And he obviously wasn't about to change his mind.

If she had felt terrible at their last meeting two years ago, now she felt a thousand times worse.

'So that's it,' she said drearily, thinking that this must be what it felt like to stand in court and hear your death sentence pronounced. 'That's all there is to say.'

'Not entirely.' Constantine surprised her by coming back swiftly. 'The question is, where do we go from here?'

'Go? Is there anywhere to go?'

'Of course.'

He sounded stunned that she should have doubted it.

'But—but you don't love me. You don't trust me. So what sort of basis do we have for any sort of relationship?'

'The perfect basis for the sort of relationship I have in mind.'

'How could you call anything that's based on the way you obviously feel about me a *relationship*?'

Constantine shrugged off the question as if it was just a petty matter, not worth consideration.

'You don't trust me, but you *want* me,' he declared with callous indifference to the distress in her eyes. 'And I don't want to feel anything for you, but I find that I'm addicted to you—physically at least. I need you; I can't live without you. You're in my blood, in my soul, and I can't get free.'

'You make me sound like some particularly nasty virus,' Grace muttered bitterly. In his blood, and in his soul—but never, apparently, where she most wanted to be: in his heart. 'I take it this "relationship" you have in mind is not meant to be permanent?'

Another of those careless shrugs indicated that he neither knew nor cared.

'I have no place in my life for a wife right now, but that doesn't mean that I want to live without a woman and all the pleasures that involves. It seems to me, *pethi mou*, that the faults that mean you are not the sort of wife I am looking for are such that would make you the perfect mistress.'

'Careful, Constantine,' Grace snapped back, using deliberate satire to hide the pain that was wrenching her heart in two. 'If you sugar-coat your proposition like that I might not fully understand exactly how sordid it is. So what, precisely, makes for a perfect mistress in your book?'

'You,' he returned, casually succinct, moving to throw himself down into one of the cream armchairs.

Leaning back easily, his hands linked together behind his head, he looked for all the world as if he actually believed that the matter had been settled, the subject closed. The arrogance of the man! Grace stormed inwardly. Did he think that all he had to do was to snap his fingers and she would fall in with whatever he had planned?

'Wouldn't you be more comfortable sitting down?'

'I don't want to sit down! I'm quite comfortable exactly where I am!' Physically at least. Mentally was quite a different matter. 'And you can't call that an answer. I want to know exactly why I would be what you term ''the perfect mistress''.'

'Isn't it obvious?' Constantine drawled lazily. 'You're a beautiful woman. You turn me on just by looking at you…'

Last night she would have taken those words as the greatest compliment; now she was no longer so sure. Hating the feel of those darkly sensual obsidian eyes on her, Grace tugged at the neckline of her robe, pulling it closed over what little skin was actually exposed.

'And you have to admit that we're sexually compatible. We only have to touch and it's like a nuclear explosion. Add to that the fact that you're bright, intelligent, classy. You have a natural style which makes you the sort of woman I would be proud to have act as my hostess, or meet my friends or business colleagues.'

'Well, thank you kindly, sir.'

Grace couldn't stop herself from dipping a mocking curtsey.

Stretching indolently, he ran one hand through the crisp darkness of his hair, looking up at her through narrowed, assessing eyes.

'We will both know exactly where we stand from now on. You understand just what it is I want from you—that and no more. And I will know that the way you feel about me, that fundamental lack of trust you have for me, will always keep you just a little on edge. Because you can never be completely sure of me, you will always feel a touch insecure. You will always be afraid that I might leave you, drop you as easily as I picked you up, and as a result you will be prepared to go to great lengths to make sure I'm happy and keep me by your side.'

'You arrogant pig!'

'And of course…' Constantine cavalierly ignored her outburst '…I shall have the peace of mind that comes from knowing that, no matter what length of time we are to-

PLAY "LUCKY 7" AND GET
THREE FREE GIFTS!

HOW TO PLAY:

1. With a coin, carefully scratch off the silver box at the right. Then check the claim chart see what we have for you — **FREE BOOKS** and a gift — **ALL YOURS! ALL FREE!**

2. Send back this card and you'll receive brand-new Harlequin Presents® novels. Thes books have a cover price of $3.99 each in the U.S. and $4.50 each in Canada, but they a yours to keep absolutely free.

3. There's no catch. You're und no obligation to buy anything. W charge nothing — ZERO — f your first shipment. And you do have to make any minimum numb of purchases — not even one!

4. The fact is thousands of readers enjoy receiving books by mail from the Harlequin Read Service®. They enjoy the convenience of home delivery... they like getting the best ne novels at discount prices, BEFORE they're available in stores... and they love their *Heart Heart* newsletter featuring author news, horoscopes, recipes, book reviews and much more!

5. We hope that after receiving your free books you'll want to remain a subscriber. B the choice is yours — to continue or cancel, any time at all! So why not take us up on o invitation, with no risk of any kind. You'll be glad you did!

YOURS FREE!

PLAY LUCKY 7 FOR THIS EXCITING FREE GIFT!

THIS SURPRISE MYSTERY GIFT COULD BE YOURS FREE WHEN YOU PLAY

LUCKY 7!

Visit us on-line at
www.romance.net

NO COST! NO OBLIGATION TO BUY!
NO PURCHASE NECESSARY!

The Harlequin Reader Service® — Here's how it works:

Accepting your 2 free books and gift places you under no obligation to buy anything. You may keep the books and gift and return the shipping statement marked "cancel." If you do not cancel, about a month later we'll send you 6 additional novels and bill you just $3.34 each in the U.S., or $3.74 each in Canada, plus 25¢ delivery per book and applicable taxes if any.* That's the complete price and — compared to cover prices of $3.99 each in the U.S. and $4.50 each in Canada — it's quite a bargain! You may cancel at any time, but if you choose to continue, every month we'll send you 6 more books, which you may either purchase at the discount price or return to us and cancel your subscription.

*Terms and prices subject to change without notice. Sales tax applicable in N.Y. Canadian residents will be charged applicable provincial taxes and GST.

gether, as long as you mistrust me I shall be free from the possible complications of having you fall in love with me.'

Now Grace did want to sit down. If she stayed on her feet, she strongly suspected that in another moment her legs would give way and she would collapse into the nearest chair. Far better to subside into it more elegantly while she still could, and so not reveal her feeling to the cold-eyed monster sitting opposite.

'You seem to have it all worked out.'

Pain made her voice cold and tight. She could only thank God that she hadn't weakened and opened her heart to him earlier. She shuddered inside to think what might have been the repercussions of telling Constantine that she was still in love with him.

'But there's one thing you haven't taken into account in your careful calculations.'

'And that is?'

'You claim that I don't trust you, but if that's the case, how do you explain the last couple of nights? Why do you think I went to bed with you? Why did I make love with you?'

For the life of her she couldn't call it having sex. She didn't care if her use of the more emotive term 'making love' gave too much away. That was what it had been to her and she couldn't describe it as anything else.

'Why did I give—give you...?'

'The gift of your virginity?' Constantine finished for her when she floundered desperately, unable to complete the sentence. 'I was honoured—what man wouldn't be? But, oh, Grace, don't delude yourself. That wasn't trust. Trust had nothing to do with it. Instead, it was the result of another, very similar-sounding word, with many of the same letters but a very different meaning.'

His words made no sense to Grace, who could only stare at him blank confusion, her brain numbed by the constant emotional battering she had taken from the moment she had woken.

'I—don't...' she began hesitantly, making him sigh impatiently.

'Obviously I mean *lust, agape mou*,' he elucidated with insulting care, as if explaining something to a not very bright child. 'Hunger, desire, passion, sex...whatever label you want to put on it. It all comes down to the same thing in the end—the sort of craving that deprives you of reason, leaves you incapable of thought.'

'No...' It was a low moan of despair, one she was unable to inject any force into.

'*Yes,*' Constantine amended sharply. 'You were completely in its grip. You couldn't shake it off, could no more deny it, say no to me, than you could have stopped yourself from breathing.'

'No...'

Grace longed to close her eyes so that she didn't have to see his dark, cruel face. She wanted to press her hands over her ears to blot out the stream of terrible, distressing words. But she knew that to do so would be tantamount to telling Constantine he was right. Even the weak denial she couldn't hold back had had the opposite effect she wanted, confirming rather than contradicting his claims.

'You can't expect me to believe that, Grace!' he scorned, leaning forward in his chair to emphasise the point, dark eyes burning as they fixed on her pale face. 'Because I was right there with you. I know exactly how it felt, because I felt it too. I'd have gone out of what little was left of my mind if I hadn't had you the night of the party, or last night, or for many more nights to come.'

'But how many more nights?'

Once more an indifferent shoulder lifted, shrugging off her shaken question.

'A hundred? A thousand? Who knows how long this fever will take to burn itself out?'

'So now I'm back to being an unpleasant infection once again!'

'You can call yourself what you like,' Constantine responded imperturbably. 'Just so long as you don't call the way you respond to me trust, or anything like it. Trust has nothing to do with it.'

'That's a very cynical interpretation of the facts.'

'Not at all. Look, I can smile and shake hands with business colleagues, or men I want to negotiate a deal with; I can work with them all day, laugh, share a meal—but I'll never, ever *trust* them. I know they're just waiting for me to slip up, show the slightest hesitation, the tiniest hint of insecurity and they'll stick the knife straight in, right in my back.'

'This isn't a business deal!'

'Isn't it?'

Constantine leaned back in his chair, steepling his long fingers together and pressing them against his lips for a moment.

'It strikes me that that's exactly what it is. A civilised trade-off.'

'Civilised!' Grace scoffed. 'You don't know the meaning of the word.'

'I believe I'm offering you a very fair exchange,' Constantine pointed out with a fiendish smile that sent shivers down her spine. 'I'll give you my time, my attention, my company. Materially, you will have anything and everything you want—you only have to ask. Your slightest whim will be answered.'

Materially. But what about emotionally? She knew she didn't have the nerve to frame the question. Deep down she already knew the answer was one that would break her heart.

So instead she forced herself to ask, 'And what would I have to give in return?'

She knew the answer to that too, and Constantine didn't let her down.

'You share my bed and my life. If I have to attend a reception, a dinner, party, you'll be there at my side. You'll come with me to the theatre, the opera, act as hostess in my home. In public you will be everything a man could want—a fantasy come true. You will be glamorous, elegant, beautiful...'

It was a long drawn-out sigh of sensual appreciation.

'So beautiful. I will dress you in the finest silks and velvet, deck you in the most precious jewels. You will want for nothing.'

Grace wished desperately that she could stop him. She didn't want to listen to this. Couldn't bear to hear the details of exactly what he wanted from her itemised in this way. But she couldn't find the strength to speak. She could only sit silently, wide-eyed and entranced, as that deep, husky, softly accented voice wove its spell over her.

'But wherever you are every man present will know that you are there with me. They will know that when the evening is over you will be going home with me. That you will be in my bed that night and every night. That I will be the man whose arms are round you and whose lips take yours. I will be the only one who makes love to you. The one who knows your body so intimately it will be like a brand on your skin. I, and I alone, will be the one who possesses your beauty.'

'Until you tire of me.'

Constantine's smile was bleak, cynical, totally without warmth.

'But if you are clever, as I believe you are, *agape mou*, then you can make sure that it will be a long, long time before your attractions begin to pall on me. So tell me, my sweet Grace, what is your answer?'

Could she do it? Could she be nothing more than Constantine's mistress? Wouldn't it be like selling her soul for a short time of pleasure? Everything inside her rebelled at the thought, nausea rising in her throat so that she had to swallow it down before she could speak.

'Grace?' Constantine prompted when she still couldn't find any words with which to answer him.

Twice she opened her mouth to say...to say what? No thought had formed in her mind, so that each time her voice failed her. She could only stare at him in blank silence, her grey eyes clouded and opaque.

'Perhaps you would like some time to think it over.'

Getting to his feet in an easy, lithe movement, Constantine checked the gold watch on his wrist, frowning as he did so.

'I really must be going. But I have booked a table at Reid's tomorrow night—for eight-thirty. I'll see you there...'

'No, you won't!' Anger pushed her upright too, standing up in a rush to face him defiantly.

His easy confidence, the total conviction that she would fall in with his plans without a murmur, was the last straw. He really believed that he could toss out a cold-blooded proposition like the one he had just detailed, one that was nothing more than a few crumbs flung casually in the direction of someone who was starving, and she would grasp it gratefully. He actually thought that when she had hoped for, dreamed of so much, she could be content with so little.

And the dreadful thing was that she was tempted. She had actually found herself considering his heartless scheme and the emotional death that went with it.

But not any more.

'I won't be coming.'

A swift on-and-off smile, brief as the flash of a neon light, mocked at her sincerity, incensing her further.

'I will wait at the restaurant for half an hour, no more...'

'You can wait till hell freezes over! I'm not coming! What you're offering isn't a relationship, it's slavery! You buy and I'm sold!'

'Grace, you do exaggerate! It's a sophisticated arrangement, one that suits many modern couples.'

'Well, it doesn't suit me! Forgive me if I'm not *modern* or *sophisticated* enough for you, but I'm not prepared to put up with it.'

'Don't give me your decision immediately.' Constantine cut across her tirade, reducing her to spluttering incoherence. 'Tomorrow night will be soon enough.'

He was heading for the door as he spoke, but just as he opened it he paused and looked back, subjecting her to a cool, narrow-eyed scrutiny.

'I shall leave the restaurant at nine exactly. If you know what's good for you, you'll be there.'

CHAPTER SEVEN

SHE *wasn't* going!

For the thousandth time since Constantine had walked out of the door, Grace repeated the command to herself over and over again.

She wasn't even going to *think* about going to the restaurant to meet him. She could be in no doubt at all that what Constantine really wanted was some sort of revenge on her for her lack of trust in him and his love for her, so was she going to help him carry out that revenge right to the bitter end?

No way! She had no intention of agreeing to his proposal, so he could sit there alone, wait his allotted half an hour alone, go home *alone*! He wasn't going to see her tomorrow night—or ever again!

And that was where her careful resolution faltered, weakening dreadfully.

How would she feel if she never saw Constantine again? After the pain, the aching loss, the sheer pointlessness of waking up day after day that she had endured the last time he had walked out of her life, could she possibly go through that again?

Could she turn her back on this one chance to keep him in her life, no matter what the conditions? And, even worse, knowing that she was the one who had put herself in this situation? That Constantine was prepared to continue a relationship with her but she had turned her back on him.

But what he was offering wasn't a relationship! Not the sort of relationship she wanted, anyway.

But she couldn't have what she wanted. The second-best

Constantine had offered her was all that was available. It was that or nothing. And she had been through nothing and knew it was like living in hell.

When she had phoned him to tell him the good news about Paula's confession he had been cold and distant. But what had worried her more was that he had refused to let her come to his apartment to explain, and had flatly rejected any suggestion that he might join her at her father's house.

In the end, the only compromise he had offered was that he would meet her at work, in the agency's main foyer. It was hardly the place for a tender, romantic reunion, but it had been the best Grace had been able to get out of him.

From the moment that he had come stalking into the room, it had been obvious that he was spoiling for a fight. His eyes had sparked with electricity, his face had been set into dangerous lines, his stance had been like that of an ill-tempered predator, bristling with aggression.

'Well?' He tossed the question at her as if he was a medieval knight, throwing down his gauntlet in challenge.

'Well, what?'

She wasn't ready for this. At the sight of him, so tall and dark and devastatingly sleek in the iron-grey suit and softer toned shirt, her thoughts had scattered here there and everywhere, and she couldn't even try and collect them together again.

'What do you want to say?'

'Isn't it obvious?' Anxiety made her edgy, her tone far too sharp.

'Not to me.'

'Constantine, please!'

This wasn't going at all the way she had expected. When she had anticipated gentleness and reassurance, his aggressive attitude rocked her sense of balance. Just what was going on here?

'Paula *lied*!' she said desperately. 'She made everything

up—she admitted it. There was no truth in anything she said.'

'And so?'

To her consternation he turned away from her, moving to the area of the foyer where comfortable chairs were provided for anyone needing to wait for their appointment. A pot of coffee was always kept warm on a hotplate, and Constantine lifted this now, gesturing in her direction.

'Drink?' he asked casually.

'No, I don't want a drink! Constantine, why are you behaving like this?'

'And how did you expect me to behave?' Constantine parried sardonically, glittering black eyes watching her closely.

'Oh, stop playing mind games!' She actually stamped her foot to emphasise her words, revealing how much on edge she was. 'I asked you here to tell you about Paula. I thought you'd be glad.'

She was subjected to a cold-eyed, cruelly assessing scrutiny that swept over her from the top of her smooth blonde head to her feet.

'Glad?' he said, his voice low and quiet but none the less bitingly emphatic. 'Glad to know that the little witch has finally told the truth? Glad to know that my name has been cleared? Why? It's of no importance.'

'No importance?' Grace couldn't believe what she was hearing. 'It's vitally important to you and me and our marriage.'

An arrogant flick of his hand dismissed her protest as totally insignificant.

'It's not even relevant,' he stated implacably.

Oh, dear God! It was as if all the whirling, conflicting emotions boiling up inside her had suddenly tangled themselves into a tight knot in her throat, making it difficult to breathe properly.

It was the quietness of his voice that did it. He hadn't even raised his tone above conversational level and yet what he'd said commanded complete attention.

'Not relevant?' she managed. 'But how…why?'

'Because there isn't going to be a marriage.'

'What? Of course there is! This was a terrible shock, but it's behind us now. It's in the past, and the future's what's ahead of us. A wonderful, bright, happy future together!'

'No way.'

At first Grace couldn't take in just what Constantine had said. The two stark, brutal syllables seemed to make no sense at all, repeating themselves over and over in her mind in a nonsensical litany that she couldn't comprehend. But then their true significance hit home like a blow to her heart.

'But, Constantine,' she cried, grabbing hold of his arm and holding on tight, 'you don't—you can't mean it!'

'I've never been more sure of anything in my life,' he returned intractably, shaking off her clinging hands with an abrupt movement. 'We are not going to be married. Not now, not ever.'

'But why…? What…?'

'Isn't it obvious?'

'Not to me!' she wailed. 'Constantine, don't do this to me. I love you!'

'No, you don't,' he shocked her rigid by declaring. 'You may have thought you did, but really you were just in love with the idea of being in love. Either that or you are even more shallow than I suspected and you were really only in love with my wealth.'

If he had taken her heart in his hands and squeezed it cruelly, she doubted if it would have hurt any more than this.

'That's a disgusting thought! I never… I couldn't…!'

Constantine shrugged off her protests with callous indifference.

'I'll give you credit for not being ruled by greed,' he conceded coldly. 'But love—no. You don't even know what the word means.'

'Of course I do!' Desperately Grace tried to will him to believe her. 'It means caring, and sharing, honesty, faithfulness, and…and…'

'And *trust*,' Constantine inserted savagely when she floundered, too terrified of the black, baleful glare he turned on her to be able to continue. 'The sort of trust that believes without question, without doubt, without thought! If you cannot trust your husband or wife-to-be, then who can you trust? And if you don't trust them, no matter what, then you have no right to be thinking of marrying them. Without trust, *pethi mou*, there is no love, and without love there will never be a marriage.'

'But I love you!' It was the only thing she could think of to say.

'You love me now—when your sister has confessed to her lies. But when I told you they were lies you wouldn't even listen. Then you were so sure you were right, so ready to believe someone else—anyone else—before me.'

'I—I didn't know.'

'You didn't need to *know*!' he flung at her. 'You only had to believe. You were incapable of that belief and so we have no future together.'

No future. The words exploded inside Grace's head, blasting her back to the present with a shock. No future.

So do you need any further evidence why you would be have to be crazy to get tangled up with a man like Constantine once again? Grace asked herself now, as the end of the day approached and she was twelve hours closer to the moment when she would have to make her decision. Did she really want to be involved with a man who could be so callous, so unfeeling, so totally unresponsive to the distress he had caused her?

'Oh, go to bed!' she remonstrated with herself, realising that it was well after midnight and she still hadn't come to any sort of a conclusion. 'Go to bed and sleep on it and things will look so much better in the morning.'

Or, rather, they might have done, if she had managed any decent sort of sleep at all. But the truth was that she had spent what remained of the night tossing and turning, unable to settle, the scene with Constantine that morning playing over and over inside her head like a film projected on to the screen of her mind.

And when she had drifted off it was to be plagued by heated, erotic dreams in which Constantine's long, hot body was tangled with her own, his hands on her skin, his mouth caressing the aching points of her breasts. So that when she woke she was wrung out and exhausted, feeling as if she had had no rest at all.

She couldn't go through it all again, she admitted. Couldn't endure the loss and the loneliness all over again. She had lived through that hell once; it would destroy her to have to endure it once again.

She hadn't been able to sway him then, and it seemed that his heart was still as implacably set against her now as it had been then. Knowing Constantine, she really shouldn't have expected otherwise.

But this time he had offered her the lifeline of a way to share his life, not as his wife, but as his mistress. It might not be the outcome she had dreamed of, but could she really turn her back on the chance to be something to him, however second-rate it might be?

It had taken just one night of deprivation, one night of doing without Constantine's touch, his kisses, his caresses, to make her admit to herself that she was addicted to him, and to his lovemaking. She couldn't live without him. It would destroy her even to try.

And he had said that it could take a long time before he tired of her. A hundred—a thousand nights.

A hundred nights were nothing. Three months and a little more. They could fly past in the blink of an eye. But a *thousand* nights...!

A thousand nights made up almost three years. That was longer than the time she had lived through since Constantine had broken off their engagement, and *that* had seemed like an eternity.

Surely in three years something could change. If she could only...

But she wouldn't let herself think about that. She couldn't allow herself to dream, because that was to risk the agony of having those dreams destroyed and losing everything she had yearned for.

She would take the little Constantine offered, for as long as he would let her. She had to. She could do nothing else. She would die if he walked out of her life now.

That moment would come, of course. One day. But right now that day was a long way ahead. Hopefully, in the intervening space of time she would grow a second skin, become strong enough to handle the inevitable when she no longer had any choice. But that was the future. What she had to deal with was the present.

And so she made her preparations for the evening ahead of her. She showered and washed her hair, blow-drying the silken strands until they gleamed like polished gold. She sprayed her body with her favourite perfume then applied a subtle make-up, emphasising her silvery grey eyes, the soft fullness of her mouth. After slipping on her newest and sexiest dress, a sleeveless Lycra tube the colour of rich clotted cream, she turned to contemplate her reflection in the mirror.

The dress clung in all the right places, emphasising and flattering the feminine curves of her body. Sheer silky stockings and delicate strappy sandals in the finest Italian leather made her legs look endless, touched with a subtle sheen. And above her wide cheekbones her eyes looked enormous, wide and brilliant, luminous with a mixture of excitement and apprehension.

Finally, as the last, finishing touch, she took the delicate bangle Constantine had given her from its padded box and slid it over her hand, letting it hang loosely around her fine-boned wrist.

There! She was as ready as she would ever be. She looked calm, elegant, supremely in control. So what if it was all an illusion? At least the tension that was tying her nerves into knots, the feeling like the fluttering of a thousand trapped butterflies beating their wings frantically in the pit of her stomach didn't show on the surface. She knew her appearance would deceive most people. Her only worry was, would it convince the person who mattered most?

Constantine was already at his table by the time she arrived. He had a drink before him, but no food. He obviously did not intend to dine alone.

As she paused in the doorway to study him for a moment she saw him push back his shirt-cuff to check the time on his watch. The small gesture made her smile secretly to herself. She had planned her arrival carefully for just this effect. She had barely five minutes left of the half an hour he had allotted her. It would do him good to be forced to wonder if in fact she was coming at all. Schooling herself to move slowly, nonchalantly, she strolled forward.

'Constantine…'

His dark head snapped up quickly, narrowed black eyes fixing on her face. So he hadn't been quite as sure of himself as he had seemed. This time her smile actually touched her lips.

'So you came.'

Impeccably polite as always, he was already on his feet, pulling out a chair for her opposite his own.

'Did you really think I wouldn't?'

She was proud of her voice. It sounded cool, light, unconcerned, which was just the way she wanted it.

'It may be cold outside,' Constantine drawled dryly. 'But I don't think it's quite bad enough to make hell freeze over just yet.'

Using the actions of shaking out her napkin and placing it on her lap to avoid having to look him directly in the face, Grace inclined her head in acknowledgement of his reference to her defiant declaration of the day before.

'It's a woman's privilege to change her mind. Surely you knew that.'

'And have you changed your opinion of the arrangement I offered? Or do you still see it as a form of captivity and humiliation?'

Grace reached for her water glass and took a careful sip in order to ease her suddenly parched throat.

'I prefer to see it as a business deal. One in which you pay handsomely for the sort of services I provide. And I intend to take full advantage of your generosity.'

'I wouldn't expect anything else.' Constantine's tone was darkly sardonic. 'That way at least we both know where we stand. So, do we shake hands to confirm our agreement?'

It was what she had come here to do, Grace told herself furiously. What she had told herself she wanted. So why should she find herself hesitating now, when the matter was all but decided?

'Second thoughts, Grace?' Constantine questioned when she sat still in her chair, unable to move.

With a struggle Grace forced a smile on to her lips, and made herself meet that searching ebony gaze head-on.

'Not at all,' she returned smoothly. 'You see, I really think that in this matter I've got the better half of the bargain.'

'In that case...'

He held out his hand and this time she was able to put her own into his, not even flinching at the inevitable sense of electrical shock as skin touched skin, palm against palm.

It was as his firm grasp closed over her fingers that she realised that the hand she held out was the one on which she wore the gold bangle Constantine had given her. And it was only now that she remembered that this particular piece of jewellery was usually described as a slave bracelet.

CHAPTER EIGHT

'GRACIE, darling, you look decidedly peaky these days! What's the problem? Is that Greek of yours not looking after you properly?'

'Not at all.' Grace switched on a smile in response to Ivan's teasing question. 'On the contrary, he's looking after me only too well.'

'Oh, I *see*.'

The exaggerated way Ivan rolled his eyes made it plain just what sort of 'looking after' he had in mind.

'No, Ivan, I do not mean sex!' This time her smile was more genuine, less forced. 'Well, not just sex! He's always giving me presents as well.'

Presents. If the truth were told, she was drowning in the things. From the very first, almost from the moment she and Constantine had come to their agreement, he had proceeded to put his half of the bargain into action—with a vengeance.

That first day he had arrived with another gift-wrapped box, much larger than the one the bangle had come in.

'I promised you something much more flattering,' he had told her. 'This is to replace the one that I ripped.'

'You don't sound exactly apologetic about it,' Grace responded, unfastening the silver and white ribbon fastened around the box.

'Apologetic?'

Arrogant black brows rose in disdain merely at the word.

'I do not apologise for destroying something less than third-rate and replacing it with something much more ap-

113

propriate. Something more suited to the beautiful woman who is to wear it.'

That *beautiful* became a two-edged sword, the huskily spoken compliment taking on another, less welcome significance, when Grace finally opened the box and carefully took out its contents.

I shall buy you a better one, he had declared, scorning the homely comfort of her towelling robe. And the simple nightdress she'd worn underneath had been ripped in two at the height of their shared passion. Now Constantine had fulfilled his promise.

But the robe and nightgown she unfolded carried a very different message from the clothing they were to replace. Made of the finest heavy silk-satin, they were blatantly, undeniably sexy. The rich, deep scarlet colour was something she would never have chosen for herself, and the simple, severe lines of the nightdress couldn't hide the fact that the neckline was slashed as low as it could go, and there was very little back at all.

It was perfectly obvious just what had been going through Constantine's mind when he'd bought them. They were the sort of clothes that a man would give to his lover. They were not meant to be worn for any length of time but simply slipped on in order to seduce and tantalise, to arouse passion mainly at the thought of taking them off again. They didn't so much scream sex as murmur it seductively, but Grace felt that if they had borne the label 'Lingerie for Your Mistress', then she wouldn't have been surprised.

'They're—lovely.' It was impossible to hide the catch in her voice, so she could only pray he would take it for excitement.

'Not as beautiful as the woman they were chosen for, Grace, *pethi mou*...' Constantine's voice deepened noticeably on the last words, his accent thickening markedly. 'Put them on. Model them for me.'

'I don't…' Grace demurred, ducking her head to avoid the burning intensity of his gaze. 'I'm not sure…'

It was one thing to agree to Constantine's terms in a rush of determined resolve at the end of two days of wavering backwards and forwards, quite another to play out the part of the mistress in cold blood, so to speak.

'Don't be shy, my Grace,' that soft, husky voice cajoled. 'You know how I feel about that glorious body of yours. And besides, there isn't a single inch of you that I haven't seen or touched or kissed…'

But that had been in the heat of passion, when she had been head over heels in love and had believed she was loved in return. It was quite, quite different from modelling this slinky sliver of silk, parading up and down before Constantine's coolly appraising eyes, knowing that all he felt for her was desire, the lust he had described to her so eloquently before.

'Constantine…I can't…'

But he took her in his arms and kissed her softly, persuasively. With calculated skill he gently woke her senses, roused the hunger that lay only just beneath the surface and brought it swiftly to clamouring, urgent life.

In the end, the nightdress and robe weren't needed. The aching need that swept over them like a tidal wave drove away any thought of hesitation or titillation. Neither was prepared to wait, to allow time for the sort of love games Constantine had originally had in mind. But later, with their need for each other temporarily appeased, Grace was persuaded to slip them on, which, of course, started the whole thing all over again…

That night had set the pattern for all the rest. By day they were both busy with their jobs, but it seemed to Grace that she was only functioning on automatic pilot, barely fully awake or aware of her world. She only truly came alive in the evenings, when Constantine sometimes took her out for a meal or to the theatre, as he had promised, but more often than not they simply stayed in her flat, in her bed.

It didn't seem to matter how many times they made love, it was never enough. Each shattering orgasm only eased the craving just long enough for them to recover, for their breathing to slow, the frantic pounding of their hearts to ease.

But even as they lay spent, their sweat-slicked bodies splayed in total abandonment on the bed, the insidious hunger was creeping through every cell, every nerve, wakening them, tormenting them until they could do nothing but reach for each other once more. In the end, only the total exhaustion that drove them into the oblivion of sleep granted them any reprieve from the incessant demands of their bodies.

'...in September. Will that be okay?'

'What?'

Blushing fierily, Grace realised that while she had been lost in her erotic memories Ivan had been speaking to her and she hadn't heard a thing.

'I'm sorry—my mind was elsewhere.'

'Obviously!' Ivan's tone was arch. 'And I can guess just where it was. Gracie, darling, you really have got it bad. And what about the gorgeous Constantine? Is he as deeply involved as you are? Does this mean we can soon expect to hear the sound of wedding bells?'

Grace shuffled a pile of papers quite unnecessarily, moving them from one side of her desk to another in order to hide the pain that question brought her. She was sure it must show in her eyes, betraying her innermost feelings to someone who knew her as well as Ivan did.

'It's a little early for that yet,' she hedged awkwardly.

'Grace, you've been back together for nearly four months

now. The first time round you'd announced your engagement by this point.'

'Yes, well, we did rather rush into it then. We want to
take things more steadily this time—be sure of what we
feel.'

The bitter irony of that remark stabbed sharply even as
she spoke. If anything, both she and Constantine were much
surer of their feelings this time round than they had been
last time. It was the conflict between those two very different emotions that kept them apart.

'So what was it you were telling me?' With a determined
effort she managed to push the misery that thought brought
her to the back of her mind. 'Something about September?'

Ivan nodded.

'The annual meet-and-greet, drinks and networking do,'
he said, referring to the yearly reception the advertising
agency held for their major clients. 'Bob Cartwright sug-
gested the last Friday in September. Will that be okay for
you?'

'Let me check... Yes, that'll be fine. I suppose that
means I shall have to spend another evening being nice to
Les Harvey.' A faint grimace twisted her soft mouth at the
thought of the unwanted attentions the owner of a furniture
chain constantly subjected her to whenever they met.
'That'll be fun.'

'Maybe by then you'll have a brand-new engagement
ring to show you're off-limits.' Ivan's laughter turned to a
frown as he saw the way colour leached from her cheeks
at his comment. 'Are you sure you're okay? Grace—you're
not...?'

'Of course I'm not!'

With what she hoped was an airy gesture, Grace waved
away the idea that she might be pregnant.

There was no chance of that. From the first, Constantine
had made his position only too clear.

'We'll have to lay down a few ground rules,' he told her bluntly, even before their meal had been served on the night she'd had dinner with him at Reid's. 'For one thing, we've been playing with fire, sexually, and that has to stop. I'll make arrangements for you to see my doctor tomorrow.'

'I have my own doctor!' Grace declared, bristling with indignation. 'If you're talking about contraception, then—'

'Of course that's what I'm talking about! Believe me, I am not usually as irresponsible and careless as I have been the past couple of days. But I never quite anticipated that things would go this far this fast. I don't need any unwanted complications.'

'That makes two of us,' Grace muttered. Of course, the woman who was not considered suitable to be his wife was in no way fit to be the mother of the next generation of the Kiriazis family. 'But how do you know it hasn't happened already?'

'You assured me it was safe.' The words were accusatory, sparking her volatile temper.

'I said I thought it was! I'm not infallible!'

In spite of the fact that her nerves quailed inside at the problems that would ensue if she did turn out to be pregnant, she couldn't help imagining it just for a moment. Just the thought of a baby, girl or boy, with Constantine's dark hair and eyes was enough to twist a knife deep into an already vulnerable heart, making hot tears sting her eyes so that she had to blink furiously to fight them back.

'All the more reason to consult Dr Carr.'

Constantine might simply have been discussing the meal they were eating, rather than the possibility that she might have conceived his son or daughter. The casual indifference of his tone had Grace gritting her teeth against the sort of outburst that would have created a very ugly scene indeed in the elegant restaurant.

'I said I have my own—'

'And I said you'll see mine!'

He hadn't raised his voice, but the forceful emphasis of his words was enough to silence Grace far more effectively than any shout.

'I promised you the best of everything while we are together, and I intend to keep that promise. As long as you are mine, you will have the finest medical attention money can buy...'

He made her sound like a prized brood mare, Grace thought bitterly. With one vital difference, though. He would want a horse to become pregnant, while he had made it plain that it would not please him if she did.

'And if there should be any repercussions from the nights we spent together—well, we'll cross that bridge when we come to it.'

Much as she wanted to, Grace didn't have the nerve to ask just what crossing that bridge might involve. When they had been engaged before, Constantine had made it plain that he wanted children very much. *That* Constantine would have welcomed the idea of a baby, whether its conception had been planned or not.

But the man who sat before her now, dark eyes hooded, his stunning features shuttered, his thoughts closed against her, was a very different prospect from the man she had so wanted to marry. *This* Constantine was an unknown quantity, and she had no idea which way he might jump if he was forced into a situation that was not to his liking.

Which still didn't stop her from being weak enough to pray that she *was* pregnant, no matter what problems that might bring. And on the morning when she woke with the familiar ache low in her body that told her her prayers had not been answered she was so desolated that she had to hurry to the bathroom to hide her misery.

Turning the shower on at full power, she stood under it for a long time, letting the rush of the water hide the tears that streamed down her cheeks until she had wept her fill and was calm enough to face Constantine again.

'I think perhaps I'd better have words with Constantine.' Ivan's voice broke into Grace's reverie, making her wonder just how long she had been wrapped up in it, oblivious to the fact that he was still standing there. 'You really are not your usual lovely self. What you need is a holiday, somewhere hot...'

'What do you feel about a holiday—somewhere hot and sunny?' Constantine said that night, making her start with surprise. 'Now what have I said?' he asked, frowning as she stared at him in bemusement.

'Oh—sorry—it's just that that's exactly what Ivan said he thought I needed. He—he said he thought I looked a bit tired... Did you have anywhere particular in mind?' she hurried on, fearful that Constantine might question her further. She could just imagine his reaction if she told him of Ivan's speculations as to exactly why she might be tired.

'I thought we could spend some time on Skyros.'

'Skyros,' Grace echoed, struggling to keep her voice even.

She had only once visited the beautiful Greek island where Constantine had been born and where his parents still had their family home. That trip had changed her life because it had been there, on a beautiful early spring evening, that Constantine had asked her to be his wife.

Just for a second, a wild, crazy thought flared in her mind, but she clamped down on it hard before it even had time to form properly, let alone take root. She couldn't allow herself to dream of another special evening, another proposal. Constantine had made it painfully clear that nothing like that lay in the future and she would only be deluding herself if she even considered it.

'Do your parents still live there?' she asked carefully,

stacking the plates they had used for their meal, ready to take them into the kitchen.

'Of course.'

Something about his casually dismissive tone rubbed the wrong way over nerves already very close to the surface of her skin.

'There isn't any ''of course'' about it!' she snapped sharply. 'We've been together now for almost four months, but we might have just met for all that I know about you. You keep me strictly on the edges of your life, giving me time only when you can spare it from the demands of your work. We only ever meet here, or in some neutral place like a theatre or a restaurant! I'm never allowed to set foot in your home...'

'I thought you wouldn't want to,' Constantine inserted harshly, stunning her into silence.

'I—I don't understand,' she managed when at last she could speak again. 'Why wouldn't I...?'

'One word,' he returned laconically. 'Paula.'

'Paula?' she echoed dazedly. 'But why?'

'Grace, I still have the same apartment that I lived in before. I assumed that you wouldn't want to set foot in the place because being there would remind you of the fight we had over... Here, let me take those!'

Moving forward swiftly, he took the plates from Grace's suddenly insecure hold, grasping them just in time before she let them drop in shock.

It was the last thing she had expected. It had never even crossed her mind that Constantine had kept her away from his apartment in order to protect her from the unhappy memories she might have of the place. If anything, she had thought that he believed that as his mistress it was her place to stay at home and wait until her lord and master could spare the time to visit her, that he didn't want his flat sullied by her presence.

'Constantine…' she said shakily. 'Tell me about Paula.'

He had taken the plates into the kitchen and she heard him deposit them on the draining board with a distinct crash. But if her question had thrown him at all, then he showed no sign of it when he appeared in the doorway again, once more completely back in control, the assured, composed man she knew only too well.

'What about Paula?'

'The truth.'

'The truth?' he muttered cynically. 'Now would that be her truth or the one you thought…?'

'Constantine! We both know she lied. But what went before that? Because there was something—I know there was.'

'You mean the way she came on to me? From the first moment we met she was all over me. I couldn't turn up at your home without meeting her on the stairs half dressed, or in some skirt that barely covered her behind. I thought I'd made it plain that I wasn't interested, but you know what they say about a woman scorned.'

'Why didn't you tell me?'

The look he turned on her was one of pure contempt.

'And you'd have believed every word?'

'If you'd told me, I would! I *would*!' she protested at Constantine's snort of disbelieving laughter.

'You didn't believe a word I said when I said I'd never seduced her.'

How she wished she could deny it, but it was only now that she realised the wrong she had done him. She should have trusted him. Should have refuted Paula's accusation at once.

'I should have believed you…' she said shakily, looking up into his darkly watchful eyes.

But even as she spoke she saw some change in his expression, the tiniest flicker of something behind the controlled mask that was all he ever showed her. In the space of a heartbeat she was transported back to that day over two years before, hearing her own angry, accusatory voice—and seeing a similar betraying reaction in Constantine's face.

It hadn't been all her own fault. It hadn't been just her lack of trust that had torn them apart. There had been something more...

'But you were feeling guilty about something that day!' she flung at him, wincing as his grip tightened on her arms.

'*Theos!* You never stop, do you?'

A stream of darkly eloquent and obviously obscene Greek left her in no doubt as to the violence of his feeling.

'Even now, even knowing your sister's part in it, you still cannot bring yourself to—'

'I *do* trust you!'

'Of course you do!' he derided, releasing her so abruptly that she was badly off balance and had to reach out hastily to steady herself against a chair. 'You can say the word so easily, *pethi mou*, but it is only a word! There is no real feeling behind it.'

'Because you won't let me *show* the feeling!' Grace protested vehemently. 'You had me tried, convicted and condemned before I even had a chance to speak! I'm only fit to be your mistress, nothing more! So what makes you the moral judge in all this, Mr Oh-So-Perfect Kiriazis? Why don't you acknowledge that you still have something on your conscience that you're not admitting to?'

Oh, *why* had she had to go and say that? Why couldn't she keep her big mouth shut and let the storm pass over her head for once? She could see Constantine's withdrawal in his face, stretching the skin tight over the sculpted cheekbones before he actually moved away from her. How she wished the foolish, unthinking words back, all the while knowing it was completely impossible.

'I think we'll forget about dinner tonight.' Each word was cold and clipped, completely without emotion. 'Perhaps we have spent too much time cooped up together. I, for one, could do with a break.'

'Constantine, no...' Grace began, but he ignored her, his face closed against her, hard and uncompromising, as if carved from granite.

'I have to go to New York on Sunday, so I'll be away for a week or so. I'll call you when I get back.'

Looking round for his jacket, he snatched it up and began pulling it on.

'Think about the holiday. When I get back would suit me—oh, here...'

Sliding one hand into his jacket pocket, he pulled out a gold-coloured box and tossed it carelessly on to the nearest chair.

'I thought you might like that.'

'Oh, Constantine, not another present!' Grace protested. 'I don't need any more jewellery.'

But she was talking to empty air. Constantine had already gone, marching from the room without so much as a kiss goodbye. The sound of the door slamming to behind him had an ominously final emphasis to it.

But at least he had said he would call. And he had told her to think about the holiday. That had to mean that he was planning on coming back. He had to come back. She couldn't have driven him away again!

Drearily she surveyed the box that lay on the cushions, her heart feeling as if it was being slowly torn in two.

Another present. Earlier that day she had felt as if she was drowning in the gifts that Constantine had brought her. Now she felt as if she was very definitely going down for the third time. Couldn't he see that there was only one thing she wanted from him?

But of course the one thing she needed from Constantine

was the one thing he was unable to give her. He didn't love her; he had made that quite plain.

Materially, you will have anything and everything you want. Inside her head she could hear Constantine's voice as clearly as if he was actually standing behind her.

Well, he'd kept his promise and been as generous as he'd said, in every way but emotionally. And it was that lack of emotional response that was slowly killing her.

'Oh, Constantine!'

Miserably she sank down on the chair and picked up the small golden box, plucking listlessly at the ribbon around it. It must have been fastened rather more loosely than she had realised because it came adrift at once, the lid falling off and its contents spilling out on to her lap. And what she saw made her catch her breath in sharp distress.

'Oh, no!'

The necklace was pure gold, obviously of the finest workmanship. It was made up of twelve separate links, and each link was in the shape of a leaf, a delicate piece of work with all the lines and veins perfectly traced out in the fine metal.

One for every month of the year.

It had been almost in the first week they had met that she had told Constantine of the superstition that if you caught a falling autumn leaf before it hit the ground, then it guaranteed a happy month for the following year. He had listened in silence, a wry smile curving his lips at the eccentricities of the crazy English people, but a few days later he had brought her a small carved wooden box that had made a strange rustling sound when she shook it.

'Constantine? What on earth...?' she had asked in confusion.

'Open it,' he had urged. 'Open it and see, *agape mou.*'

Her hands had trembled so that she had had trouble lifting the lid, but when she had she'd found herself staring at a small collection of tiny leaves, each one crisp and bright in the tawny colours of autumn. When she'd counted them, she had found that there were twelve exactly.

'One for every month of the year,' Constantine had told her. 'To guarantee that every month will be the happiest you have spent, because we will spend it together. And when that year is up I will bring you twelve more, and again at the end of the following year, for the rest of our lives. So that the time we are together will always be the happiest part of your life.'

But of course that promise had never been fulfilled. Before that first year was over Paula had spread her malicious lies, Grace and Constantine had fought, and the marriage had been called off.

'Oh, Constantine! Constantine!' Grace sobbed, holding the necklace tight against her, the tears streaming unchecked down her colourless cheeks.

She was weeping for the innocent, gentle days, when the gifts Constantine had given her had been so special, so simple, not the unwanted expensive luxuries he now showered her with. The days when she had known that she loved him and had believed that she was loved so deeply in return.

But most of all she was weeping in despair at the thought that those days had been destroyed so completely, and there seemed no hope at all of them ever being brought back to life ever again.

CHAPTER NINE

GRACE stepped into the cool of the shady hallway and sighed faintly, flexing her shoulders to ease their stiffness.

'Tired?' Constantine's keen hearing had caught her reaction and he slanted narrowed black eyes in her direction.

Wearily she nodded, wishing it was really that simple.

'It was a long journey—and it's hot!'

She plucked uncomfortably at the smart grey trouser suit she was wearing. It had been quite appropriate for London's much cooler August, but here, in the baking temperatures of the Sporades group of islands set in the Aegean Sea, it was definitely too heavy.

'You should be thankful for the helicopter,' Constantine returned dryly. 'It would have been a much longer journey if we'd come by ferry or hydrofoil. Even under ideal conditions the ferry can take up to seven hours to get here from Athens. Skyros is the most remote island in this group—that's what gives it its character.'

'It certainly has that!' Grace commented, thinking of the old men in their baggy blue trousers, black caps and flat leather sandals with many straps, the women wearing long headscarves they had passed on the way to the villa. 'Driving here was like going back in time.'

'The islanders certainly cling on to the old customs.'

'But your family didn't. You wouldn't be where you are now if that had been the case.'

'True.' Constantine nodded his dark head. 'My grandfather grabbed at the twentieth century as hard as he could. He wanted more than just this small, rugged island... Ah, Florina...'

He greeted the small, stocky woman dressed all in black who had appeared at the far end of the corridor.

'You remember Miss Vernon?'

Florina's only response was a swift duck of her head in Grace's general direction. It was only too obvious that she remembered very well, but that that memory included the way the younger woman had behaved towards Constantine, the adored only son of the Kiriazis family. Mute hostility and criticism were stamped on the blunt features.

Grace's smile faded rapidly, her small white teeth worrying at the softness of her bottom lip. She shouldn't have come. Deep down, she had known that from the start. It was impossible not to contrast her arrival today with the time she had first visited Skyros, two and a half years before.

Then she had felt as if she'd been floating six inches or more above the ground. Already head over heels in love with Constantine, she had been idyllically happy, so full of joy that nothing could have brought her down. She had adored this large, century-old stone house with its red slate roof set on the hilly coastline of a remote bay in the north of the island, and it had seemed that everyone, from Constantine's parents to the servants who tended his home, had loved her too.

But now Florina's grudging welcome had brought her hard up against how very different the reality was this time around.

'Florina!' Constantine's tone was sharp and he added something, obviously a rebuke, in stern Greek. 'Florina will take you to your room,' he added, turning to Grace. 'I'm sure you will need to rest and freshen up after travelling for so long, and I have some phone calls to make.'

That was different too, Grace reflected miserably as she followed Florina's stiffly hostile back up the polished wood staircase and across the landing, turning to the right. The last time she'd been here, Constantine had taken her to her room himself.

They had arrived while his parents were out, and he had shown her all round the house himself, almost boyish in his enthusiasm, his determination that she should see his childhood home. And when he had finally led her into the small, cool room at the back of the house, he had gathered her into his arms and kissed her thoroughly.

Clearly he had no intention of doing any such thing now. And, equally clearly, the unwelcoming Florina knew all about her change in status. The bedroom the maid led her to was not the comfortable single one, decorated in soft pastels, that she had slept in before, but a much larger one, its crisp navy and white décor uncompromisingly masculine. A room that seemed dominated by the king-size bed with a beautifully carved wooden headboard that stood in the centre.

'Your bags will be brought up here. Would you like anything to eat, *despinis*?' Florina asked stiltedly.

'Nothing, thank you—but I would like something to drink—some tea, perhaps.'

What she really wanted was to be left alone, to have a little time to think. With another silent nod the woman turned and left the room and Grace sank down thankfully on the bed. Had she made a terrible mistake in coming to Skyros?

Constantine had been distant, both physically and mentally, for the past fortnight or so. Ever since the night that she had accused him of still hiding something from her, the night when he had given her the gold leaf necklace, he had been difficult and unapproachable. So much so that she had begun to wonder.

Was it possible that the accusation she had flung at him that night had some grounding in fact? Had she touched on some nerve, ripped away some carefully protective mask that Constantine had been concealing the truth behind, and come closer to the truth than she dared admit?

But what? Paula had admitted that her story was lies, so what else could Constantine have to feel guilty about?

Unless…

Wearily, Grace kicked off her sandals and curled up on the wide, comfortable bed. Resting her head back against the soft, downy pillows, she stared up at the white-painted ceiling, lost in thought.

Was it possible that something Constantine had done, something he'd said, had given her sister the idea in the first place? Or could there have been someone else? Someone other than her sister, someone she had never suspected? Or, even worse, had her then fiancé got to her sister and forced her to say that her story had been completely made up?

No!

No sooner had the thought insinuated its nasty way into her mind than she pushed it away again. She couldn't let it take root or it would destroy her.

But Constantine had been hiding something…

The fatigue of the journey was overwhelming, sleep claiming her before she could even begin to work it out.

The sound of movement brought her slowly awake, blinking dreamily, her unfocused eyes gradually becoming aware of the long, masculine figure, casual in white polo shirt and black jeans, seated in the chair opposite the bed.

'You sleep like a child,' a soft, accented voice murmured on a note of amusement. 'Lying absolutely still, with your cheek pillowed on your hand.'

'Constantine!'

Shock had her sitting upright in a rush, confusion filling her at the thought of being observed while she had been so completely unaware.

'When did you come in?'

'I brought you the drink you asked for.'

'I would have thought that Florina…'

Constantine's beautiful mouth twisted in sardonic humour.

'I would have thought that Florina had done enough damage to your self-esteem already,' he commented with an underlying dark thread of disapproval that made Grace shiver in sympathy for the unfortunate Florina at the thought of that censure being turned on the other woman.

'She's only being loyal,' she demurred quietly, still rubbing sleep from her eyes. 'You told me yourself the Greeks are a proud race. If I offended one then I offended all.'

'Loyal and discourteous,' Constantine declared sharply. 'Whatever, I thought you would prefer it if I brought you your tea.'

A wave of one strong hand indicated the tray on the bedside table.

'Oh—I'm sorry—I must have dozed off. I'll drink—' She broke off abruptly as he shook his dark head. 'No?'

'It will be completely cold and undrinkable by now.'

'Why? How long have you been there?'

Only now did she become aware of the change in the light in the room, the shadows that spoke of the end of the day, revealing that she had slept for far longer than she had realised.

'An hour. Perhaps more.' A movement of his broad shoulder shrugged off the question.

'An *hour*!'

Grace smoothed a distracted hand over her disordered hair, struggling to collect her thoughts. She found it intensely disturbing to think of Constantine sitting there, silently watching her while she had been so unaware of his presence, so vulnerable, so exposed.

It was crazy to think that way, she knew, when all those other days and nights in her bed he had seen her wearing far less, or every bit as deeply asleep. But somehow now, with the worrying thoughts that had been preying on her mind still lingering inside her head, she found it so much more difficult to cope with the idea. What if she had talked in her sleep, murmuring something she had tried so hard to keep from him in her waking life?

'You must have been bored stiff!'

Nervously she swung her feet to the floor, hunting for her shoes.

'You should have woken me.'

'Quite the opposite,' Constantine contradicted. 'I was quite content. It was a rare opportunity to see the real Grace, the woman you—'

'I don't know what you mean.'

Uneasiness made her tone sharp. *Had* she said something? Or had some other thing, some betraying movement or gesture, given her away? Had Constantine somehow been able to read in her sleeping face the love she tried so hard to conceal from him in the daytime?

'This is the real me.'

A wild gesture swept her hands from the top of her head and down over her body, drawing his obsidian eyes with it.

'You make it sound as if I'm someone else with you— as if I'm playing a part. This *is* the real me!' she added more emphatically when the swift narrowing of his eyes seemed to question the vehemence of her response. 'What you see is what you get. If you don't like it, you can lump it.'

'Oh, I like it…' Constantine assured her smoothly. 'I like it very much. In fact…'

With a slow, indolent movement, he levered himself up out of his chair and leaned towards her. Instinctively Grace lifted her face for the kiss that she knew was coming, all her stiffness, the prickling indignation, melting away from her at the first touch of his lips.

His mouth was soft on hers, gently cajoling, the sensual slide of his tongue easing her lips apart. Strong hands tangled in her hair, holding her so close that she could smell the scent of his skin, the sun-warmed fragrance that was essentially his and his alone.

'I'd like to see so much more of you...'

Gently insistent pressure was pushing her back on to the bed and at first Grace went with it, her body limp and pliable in his hands. But then a sudden unwelcome recollection, the memory of the worries that she had been struggling with before she'd fallen asleep, had her stiffening again.

'No...' The word escaped her lips before she had time even to think about it.

It obviously surprised Constantine almost as much as it did herself to hear it.

'No?' he questioned sharply, stilling abruptly.

The swift frown that drew his dark brows together made plain his displeasure—and no wonder! Never before had she had the nerve to say no. 'No' was not supposed to come into their relationship. It was one of the unwritten, unspoken rules of their arrangement. Constantine showered her with luxuries and she provided sex on demand. And so far both of them had kept scrupulously to their share of the bargain.

'Constantine, please!' Grace said edgily, hunting for a reason that would convince him without revealing any of the concerns that were in her mind. 'I—I feel dreadful.'

Those brilliant black eyes moved over her appraisingly once again, raising stinging trails of awareness on her skin, as if they had actually touched her.

'You look fine...'

'I've been sleeping in my clothes! I feel hot and sticky

and...' She wrinkled her nose in genuine distress as she looked down at her crumpled clothes. 'And disgusting. I need a shower to freshen up.'

The silence that greeted her words stretched her already taut nerves almost to breaking point. If he said no, if he so much as kissed her again, turned on the seductive charm that she knew so well was lethal to her self-control, she would be lost. She couldn't resist him again.

But she needed time to think. Time to collect her thoughts and try to put them into some sort of order. If he made love to her now, Constantine would know something was wrong. She wouldn't be able to hide it from him. He would know, and then, if he even began to suspect that her trust in him was being questioned once again... She shuddered inside simply at the thought of his possible reaction.

'A shower...'

For a moment she was sure he was going to suggest sharing the water with her, something they had done so many times in her flat since they had become lovers. But even as she tensed, hunting for something to say that would put him off without offending him, he seemed to change his mind, pushing himself up and away from the bed.

'Fine.' The single syllable was crisp and curt to the point of coldness, speaking of a mood a million miles away from the easy composure it was meant to imply. 'You shower and change. I'll wait for you on the terrace. I'll make you a fresh drink. You must be really thirsty, having missed your tea.'

'I am.'

The look of gratitude she flashed him was heartfelt, but even as she directed it at him she felt her own change of mood. Perversely, now that he had moved away, she felt the loss of the warmth of his body, the touch of his lips, like an ache deep inside. Her skin hungered for his caress, her mouth for his kiss.

She didn't care what he had felt guilty about—if in fact he had felt any such thing! She only knew that without the solid strength of his body close to hers she felt lost, totally bereft, alone in a very disturbing way.

'Constantine…' she managed, her voice just a thin thread of sound.

But he didn't appear to have heard her whispered entreaty, or if he had he chose to ignore it.

'I'll see you in—what? Half an hour?' He was moving towards the door as he spoke.

'Th-that should do fine.'

Call him back, an insidious little voice inside her head whispered provocatively. Call him back! Tell him you've changed your mind!

She wanted to. She even opened her mouth to say the words, then closed it again, ignoring the hungry protests of her yearning senses as she watched Constantine stride from the room, handsome dark head held arrogantly high, not sparing her a backward glance.

Grace stripped off the crumpled trouser suit and hurried into the shower. Turning the water on to full power, she stood under its pounding force, willing it to drive away her fears and anxieties in the same time that it washed off the dirt and stickiness of the day.

But it did no good. Ten minutes later, although her body was clean and refreshed, her mind was still clogged by disquiet and uneasiness. A feeling like the fluttering of trapped butterfly wings started up inside her stomach as she pulled on a sleeveless dress in a pale pink soft cotton, brushed a single coat of mascara on her long lashes and a slick of lipgloss over her mouth.

It was too hot for any proper make-up, she told herself, surveying her reflection in the mirror. But the wide, apprehensive, shadowy grey eyes that stared back at her told a very different story.

'If you're honest,' she told herself severely. 'You'll admit that all this pretence is tying you in knots!'

The truth was that she felt so nervous about the prospect of facing Constantine again that she couldn't trust her hands not to shake. She felt sure that she would smudge any make-up she tried to apply, or put it on so heavily that she would look like a clown at a children's party.

The butterflies in her stomach seemed to have fluttered up into her throat, almost choking her, by the time she made her way out to the terrace at the back of the house. Constantine was there waiting for her, leaning against the stone parapet at the edge of the flagged floor. His strong back was towards her, his dark head averted as he stared out towards the horizon where the sun was slowly beginning to sink downwards towards the night.

'Con…'

Grace found her voice was weak and unsteady, croaking embarrassingly so that she had to swallow hard before she could complete his name.

'Constantine,' she managed, still unevenly, but at least it was audible this time.

She didn't know what she'd expected to see in his face, in the jet-black pools of those deep-set eyes when he turned to face her. She only knew that it wasn't the easy calm, the smiling sociability that he seemed to be able to turn on at the flick of a switch. Suspicion, hostility, anger even, these she had been prepared for, but not this relaxed, casual man who strolled towards her without a hint of hesitation.

'Feel better now?' he enquired.

'Much!' The butterflies in her throat made her breathless. 'I hate sleeping in my clothes. You feel so dreadful afterwards.'

'The journey must have taken more out of you than you realised.'

If his reaction to her arrival had been disconcerting, then

the brief, almost indifferent kiss that he brushed over her freshly washed hair was even more bewildering. They might have been strangers who had met only a short time before, mere acquaintances, not the passionate, unrestrained lovers who had shared a bed and been intimate with every secret part of each other's bodies over the past four months.

But of course she had forgotten about that fierce, burning pride of his. A pride that, once she had seemed to reject him in the slightest way, would not allow him to make any further advances again. And now that pride had made him determined to act as if nothing had happened, so he had switched on his best social manner, the smooth public veneer that hid any private feelings from the world.

'I thought you would like something cool to drink now.' A wave of his hand indicated the bottles of wine and mineral water that stood on a table nearby. 'But if you still prefer tea, I can ring for Florina.'

'No, there's no need for that. Some sparkling water would be wonderful, thank you.'

If she had sounded stilted before, it was much worse now. Even her footsteps seemed stiff and unnatural as she made her way to the edge of the terrace. Leaning on the wall where he had been when she had arrived, she looked out at the gardens that sloped away from the house, leading down to the beach and the Aegean Sea. In the daytime it was a clear turquoise-blue, but now its softly lapping waves were gilded by the light of the evening sun.

Behind her she could hear the faint hiss of a bottle being opened, the clink of ice on glass, and the gurgling sound of the water pouring into the glass. But she couldn't turn because a cold hand seemed to have reached out and gripped her heart, twisting it mercilessly.

It had been in just this place that Constantine had proposed to her. He hadn't gone down on one knee, of course, that Kiriazis pride was too strong for that, but he had produced the most beautiful diamond ring and, with his voice husky with emotion, had said...

'Grace...'

For the space of a couple of heartbeats she didn't know if the voice she heard was in the past or the present. It was only when Constantine repeated her name again that she realised he had come up behind her. Whirling round nervously, she almost knocked the fine crystal glass from his hand.

'Oh, I'm sorry! I was miles away!'

'Obviously.' His tone was dry. 'You always were fascinated by the sea,'

Did he truly believe that it was only the sight of the *sea* that had held her so absorbed? Did he not remember that special night, the feelings they had shared? Obviously not.

But then, of course, he must have visited this house many times in the past two and a half years. It was more than likely that familiarity had bred contempt, any residual pain that the emotive location brought back being worn away by the passage of time.

If, of course, he had felt any such thing. Hastily Grace sipped at her drink to cover her disturbed reaction, finding it difficult to force the cool liquid past the tight knot in her throat. Wasn't it more likely that her own foolish actions, her weak lack of trust, had destroyed the love he had felt for her so completely that he would be totally indifferent to this place that had once been so magical to her?

'If—if you lived in London all the year round, then you'd love to see the sea as well,' she managed unevenly, grateful for the excuse to turn back to stare at the waves and so hide the bitter tears that burned in her eyes. 'I can't wait until tomorrow when I can go down to the shore and actually get into the water.'

'Why wait?' Constantine surprised her by saying. 'There's plenty of time before dinner is served. Oh, not for a proper swim, perhaps, but you can always dip your toes in the surf.'

'I'd love that!'

Impulsively she held out her hand to him, and to her delight he took it, removing the glass from her grasp and placing it on the wide stone balustrade before leading her to the steps that led down from one side of the terrace.

Dusk was just beginning to gather as they made their way down the slope, thickly planted with fruit trees and pines. The flowers that had bordered the path on her previous visit in the spring were gone now, shrivelled by the burning sun, the ground beneath their feet baked brown. Their footsteps were silent, the only sound the gentle lapping of the waves against the shore.

Reaching the tiny cove, Grace immediately slipped off her sandals and dashed across the pebbly beach towards the water. With a sigh of delight she let the small waves wash over her feet, the foamy spume breaking softly over her skin.

'You look like a child!' She couldn't tell if the note in Constantine's voice was one of amusement or remonstrance, but she didn't care.

'Perhaps the Turn Back the Clock party worked after all,' she laughed, and knew her words to be a mistake as soon as she saw his face change, all the warmth leaching from it, leaving it hard and distant.

Did he think that she was angling for the chance to truly go back in time? That she was hinting at a possible return to the time when they had last been on Skyros together, when they had been so secure in the knowledge of each other's love that he had proposed, begging—no, *insisting*—Constantine Kiriazis never begged—that she should be his bride as soon as was humanly possible?

Oh, if only they could! If only it was possible to return to those happier, innocent days! But of course it could never be. A strong dose of reality had been injected into her life, destroying all the dreams of happiness she had had then.

'I feel like a child!' she improvised hastily. 'And this feels wonderful! So cool and refreshing! You should try it... Come on, Constantine!' she urged when he held back, looking reluctant. 'Let your hair down for once!'

Still he looked reluctant. Inspired by some wicked little imp of mischief, Grace bent down and scooped up a couple of handfuls of the salty water. As soon as Constantine came within range, she flung them in his direction, spattering the immaculate white polo shirt with wet drops.

'Hey! What the...?'

She had barely a second's grace. Kicking off the canvas shoes that he wore with no socks, he paused only to remove the gold watch from his wrist and stuff it into a protective pocket before he came after her, splashing water in her direction as he ran.

Shrieking in delight, Grace turned and fled, dashing through the waves, heedless of the way that the hem of her dress was getting soaked as she ran. At first she went as fast as she could, making it seem as if she wanted to put as much space as possible between herself and Constantine, but then, slowly, she let him gain on her. A few minutes more and he was right behind her, one strong arm reaching out and grabbing hold of her, bringing her swinging round to face him.

'You little witch!'

Giggling and struggling, she was swung off her feet and carried away from the sea, up on to the powdery sand. Once they were away from the water, Constantine tumbled her down on to the ground and came down after her, the heavy weight of his body covering hers as his hard lips captured her still laughing mouth, driving her giggles back down her throat.

'You are a temptress!' he muttered when at last he drew in a much needed breath. 'What man could resist you? You are beautiful and cool as the moon, yet wild as the sea.'

She felt wild at this moment. Wild and uninhibited, as elemental as the waves breaking against the shore, the sand against her back.

Constantine's mouth ravaged hers again, his hands hot and urgent as they moved over her body. The pink dress was rucked up around her waist and it didn't take him long to discover that a delicate pair of white lace briefs was all she wore underneath it. Moments later that fragile barrier too had been ripped away and tossed carelessly aside.

Grace didn't care. All the inhibitions, the worries of earlier in the day had been swept aside, washed from her as if she had actually been submerged in the sea that lapped just inches away from them. She wanted this, wanted it with a hunger that was hot as the sun, a hunger that had her lifting her hips eagerly, encouraging the hard, powerful thrust of his body into hers.

This was who she was, what she had been born for. She loved Constantine, she had always loved him, and she could do nothing at all to release herself from the golden fetters that bound her to him. But as she clung to Constantine, her nails digging into the tightly clenched muscles of his back, as the passion flared and spiralled out of control her last rational thought was that she never, ever wanted to be free from this glorious, sensual slavery.

CHAPTER TEN

'ANY particular plans for today?' Grace enquired lazily, stretching luxuriously in the warmth of the morning sun beating down on the terrace.

The day had begun in the same way as every one since they had come to Skyros, with a late awakening followed by an even later breakfast. The latter was the result of Constantine's insistence on never letting her out of bed until he had made love to her with a thoroughness that left her limp and satiated, unwilling to move ever again.

So now, lingering over a light meal of crusty bread, creamy Greek yoghurt, peaches, melons and honey, she felt as idle as a cat lying in the sun.

'Well, I had considered a swim, a little sunbathing, perhaps a light snack. After which I will definitely need a siesta.'

The glint in his eyes as he slanted a wicked, sidelong glance in her direction told her exactly how he planned to spend that siesta, and that he had no intention of wasting any of the precious time on *sleep*.

'Then dinner tonight…some wine…'

'A packed schedule, then,' Grace commented dryly.

She was finding it difficult to adjust to the man Constantine had become in the days they had spent on Skyros. He seemed to have shrugged off his role as the archetypal workaholic and become someone else, growing more relaxed and indulgent as each day passed, his mood improving as steadily as his native sun gradually darkened the natural tan of his skin to a deep, burnished bronze.

Looking at him now as he lounged back in his seat, the

sun making his dark hair gleam and gilding the skin exposed by the vee neck and short sleeves of his black tee
shirt, she thought that if she was a contented cat then he
was a sleek, sun-warmed panther, indolent and sensual.

'Well, what else is there to do here?' Constantine
drawled easily. 'This is such a tiny island, and we've visited the major tourist attractions—the beaches, the tavernas,
Rupert Brooke's grave...'

Grace nodded, recalling the trip to Tris Boukes, at the
southernmost point of the small island, where the famous
poet lay buried in what was officially now six feet of British
soil. There, she had been enchanted by the sight of the
Pikermies, the herd of tiny wild ponies, native to Skyros,
who roamed freely across the barren countryside.

'You're forgetting Skyros town itself,' she pointed out.

She had enjoyed exploring the island's main town, where
the white houses were stacked almost on top of each other
along the steep, narrow, pedestrian-only lanes and steps.

'The woodwork was just amazing.' Her eyes lit up with
enthusiasm for the beautifully hand-carved furniture on sale
in the folk-art shops. 'I could have spent a fortune there.'

'My paternal grandfather started out as a woodworker,'
Constantine astounded her by saying. 'He made much of
the furniture in this house.'

'I didn't know that!

If the truth was told, Constantine had never been exactly
loquacious on the subject of his family. She knew that his
grandfather had been born on Skyros, as had his father and
Constantine himself, and that although he had come from
humble beginnings he had been the founder of the now
multi-million Kiriazis Corporation. But never before had
Constantine opened up about him.

'So how did he...?'

'Make his fortune?'

Constantine pushed both hands through the black silk of his hair, stretching luxuriously.

'He worked harder and longer than anyone else. Invested what he earned first in educating himself, and then in buying first a small guesthouse and then later his first hotel. It was close to the port at Linaria, perfect for travellers arriving on the ferry, so it turned into a little goldmine. With the profits from that he bought another...and the rest is history.'

'Is he still alive?'

Constantine shook his head, regret clouding the brilliance of his eyes.

'He was already sixty when I was born. He died four years ago.'

'But he meant a lot to you?' It was obvious that he had cared deeply for the old man. His feelings were etched into his face, the set of that finely carved mouth.

'He was a character—strong, wise, generous...'

Long, tanned fingers touched the gold watch on his wrist, his faint smile gently reminiscent.

'He gave me this. It was my twenty-first birthday present—but I had to earn it.'

'Working as a waiter in one of the hotels?' Grace guessed, her perspicacity acknowledged by the slight inclination of his head. Now she understood why he never let the watch out of his sight, why he always took such great care of it. 'I wish I'd been able to meet him.'

That brought those ebony eyes swinging up to her face, the momentary softness fading rapidly, leaving them suddenly disturbingly cold and distant.

Of course, she thought uncomfortably. If Florina, who was only the family's maid, treated her as a pariah because of the way she had behaved towards Constantine, then naturally his grandfather, the patriarch and founder of the Kiriazis dynasty, would hardly welcome her into his home.

But then another thought struck her, one that had her mouth opening on a soft gasp of shock.

'Your grandfather was a woodcarver. Then that box...the one with...'

'He made it,' Constantine finished for her, not needing her to explain that she meant the decorated box which had contained the twelve autumn leaves he had once given her.

'I never knew...'

She had never realised that he had given her something so very special. Something that meant so very much to him personally.

'W-would you like it back?'

The blazing look that seared over her was savage in its rejection of any such idea. Constantine didn't need to use words to emphasise just how even to think of doing any such thing made him feel.

'It was a gift,' he stated harshly. 'I do not ask for my presents back.'

She'd caught that ferocious pride on the raw once again, destroying the peaceful atmosphere of earlier in the morning. The lazily contented panther was no more. Instead, he was bristling with hostility, reining in his black temper only with difficulty.

Desperately she cast about, looking for some other topic of conversation to distract him.

'You never told me—how did your parents take the news of the cancellation of our wedding?'

Oh, Lord, no. That was even worse! Why couldn't she engage her brain before putting her mouth into gear? The golden fire of anger was still there in his eyes, only now the flames were freezingly cold, shards of pure ice in the inky depths.

'They were shocked, naturally, and angry,' he stated, glacially distant, the bleak cynicism of his tone having the bite of concentrated acid, making her wince painfully deep inside.

'At me?'

A swift frown drew together the dark brows, Constantine's glance in her direction expressing incredulity that she should even ask the question.

'At *me*,' he corrected tightly.

Grace knew she was staring, shock and disbelief showing in her eyes.

'At you? But why? I mean, I was the one who...'

'You were the one who postponed the wedding—but I was the one whose actions seemed to be responsible for that. If I had been unfaithful to my bride even before we were married, then such behaviour would cast a terrible slur on my family's honour.'

'But surely they didn't believe...' She saw the yawning trap gaping wide at her feet just too late to stop herself from blundering right into it.

'My fiancée believed accusations that had been made...' The savagery of the statement tore at her heart for all that it had been expressed in a flat, emotionless tone. 'So naturally they were afraid that there was more evidence of those accusations than at first appeared. But when I assured them—'

'You assured them!'

Wonderful, gloriously liberating anger boiled up inside Grace's mind, freeing her from the shock and concerned guilt that had had her in their grip only moments before.

'You *assured* them!' she repeated, lacing each word with corrosive sarcasm. 'Oh, that's just great! You explained things to your parents, assured them there was no truth behind Paula's stories, but you left me floundering.'

'If you remember rightly, I did try,' Constantine inserted coldly. 'I shouldn't even have needed to do that when you claimed to love me.'

'Your mother loves you!'

'My mother loves me, but she is also realistic. She knows that since I became a man, my private life has been exactly that—private. I do not discuss my sex life with her any more than she would discuss hers with me.'

Grace winced away from the blunt brutality of the *sex life* that reduced their relationship to the purely physical, with nothing of the emotional in it at all.

'She needed me to tell her—'

'*I* needed you to tell me! Yes, I know I was angry, but you must have seen how upset—and how afraid I was. You could have tried harder to convince me of the truth.'

'And *you* should have laughed in your sister's face. You shouldn't have believed for one second that her stories had any credence!'

Pushing back his chair with an ugly scraping sound on the stone-flagged floor, Constantine got to his feet and moved to the edge of the terrace, bracing his arms on the stone parapet as he looked out at the sea.

Behind him, Grace could only stare miserably at the long, straight back, narrow hips and long legs in well-cut chinos, every inch of them taut with aggression and rejection. Even angry and distant from her, as he was now, he still had a forcefully sensual impact that was like a mule's kick in her stomach.

She longed to go to him, slide her arms around that narrow waist, press herself close up against the hard length of his body and just hold him until slowly, unwillingly perhaps, he softened, turned, took her in his arms...

No! What was she thinking of?

Oh, she could bring him out of his present vicious mood easily enough. She could entice him out of it using the wild sexual pull that their bodies had for each other, like the most powerful, irresistible magnets. She could seduce him into making love to her and so forgetting this disturbing confrontation, satiate his body so that his mind was incapable of thought. But it would be no answer. When they woke later today, or tomorrow, the problems would still be there.

'So it was a test.'

As she spoke she realised that she still held the piece of bread she had picked up long minutes ago, just before she had asked him about his parents. Now it was crushed and ruined by her convulsive grip, crumbling into nothing as she slowly released it.

'A test that it seems I failed.'

Slowly Constantine turned back to face her, resting his lithe hips against the stone wall, his tanned arms folded across his broad chest just as they had been more than two years before, when he had confronted her over Paula's accusations.

'I think we were both testing each other, Grace,' he stated flatly. 'And perhaps in our own ways we both failed.'

And then, while she was still digesting that, trying to work out exactly how he had meant it, he seemed to shrug off the black mood that had enclosed him. The coldly withdrawn look vanished from his face as if wiped away with a cloth as he stood upright again, straightening his shoulders.

'Well, if we are to go down to the cove you will need to change into something more casual. And don't forget the sun cream. I wouldn't want that beautiful skin to burn. We'll meet back here in—say half an hour?'

He didn't wait for an answer, obviously taking her acquiescence for granted as he strode back inside the house.

Left alone, Grace could only stand and stare. Was that it? Could he really just shrug it off like that—water under the bridge? Well, one thing was for sure: she couldn't!

But now was not the time to go after him, try to have it out with him. She'd seen Constantine in this sort of mood often enough to know that to push him would only make him dig his heels in even harder. She might as well batter her bare hands against a brick wall as try to talk to him in this intractable frame of mind.

So she would follow his lead—for now. She would continue with their holiday, go swimming, sunbathe. She would let him think that he could have everything his own way, until it suited her to do otherwise.

And then, at some point when he least expected it, she would tackle him about the enigmatic statement he had made. And this time she would want some answers.

After such an inauspicious start, the day went surprisingly well. It followed exactly the pattern Constantine had mapped out: the refreshing swim in the sun-warmed sea, sunbathing in the privacy of the cove. And then, in order to escape the blazing heat of the middle of the day, they retired to the bedroom, cool and air-conditioned behind closed shutters.

And in the bedroom it was as it always had been. Constantine had only to take her in his arms, kiss her with the special magic that only he possessed, and all thought of the morning's confrontation melted from her mind like a mist before the sun. She could only abandon herself to the sensual mastery of his touch, the skilful enchantment that awoke all her senses one by one until she was just a molten, mindless creature moaning her need in his arms.

But there was something new this time. Something that made their lovemaking more urgent, more hungrily passionate than ever before. With her thoughts too hazed by drugging need, her body on fire, the spiralling yearning completely out of control, Grace had no way of knowing just what it was that was different. It was only when the long, carnally hedonistic afternoon was over, when exhaustion rather than repletion forced them into sleep, that she managed to wonder if the things he had said that morning had anything to do with it.

Perhaps in our own ways we both failed.

The cryptic comment was the last thing in her thoughts when sleep claimed her, the first when she woke again.

The day had slipped away unnoticed; already the earliest signs of dusk were beginning to gather. At her side Constantine still slept, his stunning features relaxed, long thick lashes lying in jet-black arcs above the wide cheekbones.

Her thoughts preoccupied, Grace slipped from the bed and went through the usual routine of showering and washing her hair. She put on a simple soft green dress, preparing for the evening meal they would share. But all the time her mind was buzzing, thinking back, considering, wondering.

We both failed. Had the arrogant, implacable Constantine Kiriazis actually admitted to being in the wrong? Never! But it had sounded as if he was at least making a concession.

She was out on the small balcony letting her blonde hair dry in the weakening sun when she finally heard Constantine stir and head for the shower himself.

He had loved her so much before, she reflected, recalling the moment when he had given her the box of autumn leaves. But what did Constantine truly feel for her now? It was said that the opposite of love was hate, but she didn't think that quite fitted. She wouldn't be here, on his beloved Skyros, in the family home, if that were the case.

But perhaps the real truth was that the opposite to love was *nothing*. That all Constantine really felt was the blazing physical attraction that he had declared so openly, and nothing more. And yet he had loved her once. Was she only fooling herself to dream that perhaps one day that love could be revived?

A light touch on the back of her neck made her jump

like a startled cat. A moment later she felt the warm pressure of Constantine's lips on her skin, just above the fastening of the gold leaf necklace.

'A penny for them,' he murmured, coming to her side, dark and devastating in a crisp black shirt and black trousers.

'Seeing as we're in Greece, shouldn't that be a drachma for them?' Grace hedged nervously, trying to collect her scattered thoughts into something she could tell him so that she didn't blurt out the truth. 'But if you must know I was wondering how you ever manage to leave this island. It's going to be such a wrench when I have to go.'

Which she would have to inevitably—and soon. The holiday was drawing to a close. A couple of days more and they would be heading back to England.

'It isn't easy,' Constantine admitted. 'But there's always the thought of coming back.'

The thought of him coming back, or both of them? Grace found that the question meant too much to her to be able to find the courage even to ask it.

'We'll talk about it over dinner. That and other things.'

'What other things?'

But Constantine simply shook his head and, taking hold of her hand, led her out of the room.

'Later,' was all he said. 'We'll eat first. I, for one, am ravenous.' The look he slanted in her direction had a wicked, teasing glint in it. 'Anyone would think I had been doing something active this afternoon, instead of just lolling in bed.'

When he looked at her like that she could almost convince herself that he felt more for her than he admitted. With those piercing dark eyes softened by a trace of warmth, a slight smile curving his lips, he was so much closer to the Constantine she had known at first. The man who had brought her here to his island home to ask her to marry him.

Grace's heart lurched so violently that she almost missed her footing on the stairs. Could it happen? Could those 'other things' he wanted to talk to her about include the possibility that he was planning to repeat their private history and propose all over again?

It was not a thought that made for a relaxed state of mind, as a result of which her appetite totally deserted her. She could only pick at her food, pushing the tasty dish of stuffed aubergines around on her plate. Constantine too seemed absorbed in his own reflections, only coming out of them briefly when a phone rang inside the house.

'Shouldn't you answer that?' Grace asked when he didn't move.

'Florina will get it. If it's important, she'll come and fetch me.'

It was the longest speech he had made for some time, after remaining taciturn and withdrawn, his answers to the few questions she had formed monosyllabic and vague.

In the end, Grace could stand it no more.

'Constantine...'

But she got no further. Even as she spoke the door swung open and Florina stomped in, blatantly ignoring Grace as she directed a flow of incomprehensible Greek at Constantine. Seeing his swift frown, the way he snapped out a couple of sharp and obviously probing questions, she felt anxiety twist in her stomach. And when she caught a couple of words she actually understood her concern grew.

'What is it? Constantine, what's happening?'

She was ignored as he issued a string of instructions to the maid, and only when Florina had left the room did he direct his attention back to her.

'Is something wrong? I heard the words *mitera* and *pateras*—your mother and father—what's happened to them?'

'Nothing has happened. It is simply that my parents have telephoned to say that they are coming here tomorrow. I was not expecting them so soon. They had been staying with my sister in Athens, but for some reason they have cut short their visit.'

The sense of release from tension was like a rush of adrenaline, making her smile her relief straight into his dark eyes.

'But that's wonderful! I'd love to see them both again!'

But something was wrong. No answering smile softened Constantine's face. Instead he seemed even further away from her than before, every muscle in his face tight, black eyes hooded, his mouth clamped into a hard, unyielding line.

'I am afraid that will not be possible.'

'Not possible! But why?'

'We are leaving Skyros tonight.'

Grace's head went back slightly, her grey eyes widening in shock.

'And just when was this decided? We have nearly three days...'

'The holiday is over.' It was brutally autocratic: a decree issued by a tyrannical ruler to his lowly subject. 'The helicopter will take us to Athens airport. My plane will be waiting for us there.'

'But I don't want to go! I won't—'

'You have no choice!' Constantine snapped. 'It is already decided.'

'Yes, by you! But what about me? I demand some sort of an explanation. I don't want to be rushed off like this. I would like to see your parents again.'

'But they would not want to see you.'

Fired by indignation, Grace had been pushing herself to her feet, but now she subsided back into her seat, feeling as if a cruel blow had just driven all the breath from her body. The wash of angry colour leached from her face, leaving it ashen pale.

'W-what?'

'My parents would not wish to see you,' Constantine repeated implacably. 'And I would not want you to see them. I have never made it my habit to introduce my parents to any of my mistresses. That is an honour I reserve solely for the woman I intend to make my wife.'

Which left her completely without a leg to stand on. Feeling as if she was coming to pieces inside, Grace knew that the only option left to her was to get out of this with as much dignity as she could manage.

Blinking back the tears that burned at her eyes, determined that Constantine should not see them, she forced herself to keep her expression as cool and indifferent as his as she rose to her feet.

'I'll go and pack, then.'

She was proud of her voice. It sounded perfectly controlled, revealing no trace of the explosive mixture of violent emotions roiling savagely in the pit of her stomach.

'Florina is already doing that. I told her to have your cases ready as soon as possible.'

With an imperious gesture he indicated the meal on the table, her barely touched plate.

'You still have time to finish your dinner.'

But that was just too much. Drawing herself up to her full height, Grace looked him straight in the eye, her chin lifting defiantly.

'There is nothing to finish,' she told him. 'If I ate another mouthful it would choke me. I have had more than enough of it—and of you.'

CHAPTER ELEVEN

'DO YOU ever intend to speak to me again?'

The journey from Skyros to London, and its final stage back to her own home, had been completed before Grace could bring herself to speak to Constantine at any length.

Since the moment she had walked away from him and the remnants of their meal, every action she had taken had been performed in almost total silence. She hadn't even been able to bring herself to look at him, but had sat first in the helicopter, then the plane and finally in the luxurious chauffeur-driven car that had met them at the airport with her face carefully averted, staring stonily out of the window, seeing nothing.

She hadn't even felt very much. Shock seemed to have numbed her brain so that no emotion could take root. This must be how it felt to lose a limb in an accident, when the trauma was so great that for a long time the mind simply refused to accept that it had happened and so felt no pain.

'What is there to talk about?' she asked drearily as Constantine dropped her bags to the floor of her sitting room in evident annoyance. 'I think you've already said everything there is to be said. You've certainly made your opinion only too plain.'

'You knew what the arrangement was when you went into it,' he stated callously.

Yes, she had, and then she had thought she could handle it. But not any more. She had told herself that being with him was worth any price, but now she was paying far too much for the pleasure of simply having him near. It hurt too much knowing that he would never love her—and if she had had any doubts on that score, then his behaviour before they had left Skyros had driven home the truth with a sledgehammer.

But how would she live without him? It seemed to her that she risked leaping out of a very hot and torturous frying pan into an even hotter and very much more dangerous fire. She couldn't live with either situation but she had to choose one, even if it tore her heart and her mind apart to do so.

'I knew what you wanted from the relationship! The rules you were at such pains to lay down that I should follow!'

She knew from his swift dark frown that her tone and her words were a mistake, but she couldn't find it in her desolated heart to care. Suddenly the dam that had been holding back her feelings ever since the island had burst, and the words flooded out with a vengeance.

'You told me how I should live my life, what I should wear, how I should behave. You ruled my days with your occasional calls, your late, late visits, and your insistence that I should be available when you wanted—and exclusively to you! You ruled my nights with your—your sexual demands, the satisfying of which was all that you thought I was fit for! You practically told me what to eat, when to sleep—how to breathe! You took over my existence and now I want it back!'

'You don't mean that!'

'Oh, so now you've taken over my mind as well, have you? Well, let me tell you that this time your telepathic powers have let you down.'

In a gesture that mirrored her inner turmoil, she pulled off the white linen jacket she was wearing and tossed it angrily on to a nearby chair, wishing she could jettison her emotional distress at the same time.

'Because I do mean it, Constantine! I mean every word. I want you out of my life, right now, and—'

'You don't... *Theos!*' Violently he corrected himself, shaking his dark head in frustrated fury as he did so. 'Grace you *can't* mean this!'

From her defensive position on the far side of the room, Grace could only stand and stare, blinking in sudden confusion. She almost expected to see that Constantine had vanished in a puff of smoke and someone else had appeared to take his place.

Because something had happened in the last few seconds: something she couldn't yet be quite sure of and something she couldn't begin to interpret.

For one thing, part-way through that last declaration Constantine's voice had changed dramatically. It had ceased to be the arrogant, inflexible set of commands that was typically Constantine, and had become instead something that sounded unnervingly like a—a...

When Grace hunted for words to describe it, the only one she could come up with was an entreaty.

And in the same moment something had come over Constantine's face. Something desolate and bleak that dulled the brilliance of his eyes, filling them instead with turbulent shadows like the clouds that gather on the horizon in advance warning of a violent storm.

'What did you say?' Suspicion and uncertainty blended together on the question.

Sighing deeply, Constantine raked both hands through his hair, his bruised-looking gaze fixed on her face.

'I said you can't mean this. You can't end it now.'

'I can do whatever I want.'

'But, Grace, *agape mou...*'

'Don't call me that!'

Throwing aside her jacket had been a definite mistake. She was still wearing the green dress she had put on for dinner at the villa, a dress that had been suitable for the much warmer conditions of Greece. Here, on a typically rainy late summer English night, the temperatures had dropped considerably, so that her exposed skin felt chilled and clammy. She had to struggle against the need to rub her hands up and down her arms to ward off the shivers.

Constantine, on the contrary, looked supremely comfortable. The lightweight jacket he wore over his black shirt and trousers was much more protection against the cold. It was one more thing to hold against him, and she tried to inject all the resentment and anger she could into her feelings. At this moment hate was so much safer than love.

'If you call me that again, I swear I'll kill you! *Agape mou!*' she echoed cynically. 'My love—my *love*! You don't even know what the word means!'

'I know what it means to me,' Constantine snarled. 'It means that I cannot let you go. That without you I can't sleep, I can't work, I can't *live*! Without you my life is empty, unendurable! I have had more than two long years of that and I will not take any more!'

There was a roaring, booming sound inside Grace's head. Her heart was pounding so hard that her blood was thundering through her veins, making her feel dizzy and faint so that she had to reach out to a nearby chair for support. Drawing a deep breath, she forced herself to speak.

'I don't know if you realise what you said then, Constantine.' It was a struggle to keep the words calm and even and not gabble them out in a desperate rush to ease the tension inside her head. 'But it sounded remarkably like a declaration of love.'

Her words fell into a stunned silence that dragged on and on, stretching her already over-sensitised nerves almost to breaking point. She felt as if all that had gone before had flayed off a protective layer of skin, so that she was even more vulnerable to what was to come, too scared even to hope.

'Constantine…' she prompted fearfully when he didn't speak.

The man before her stirred slowly, as if waking from a long, drugged sleep. Briefly he closed his eyes, and when he opened them again it seemed to Grace that they were focused on something else, something far, far away.

'Love,' he echoed cautiously, as if testing the word, his mouth twisting on the sound. 'Love—well, yes, what the hell, why not admit it?'

It was impossible to believe what she was hearing.

'You love…'

Suddenly it was as if someone had flicked a switch inside Constantine, driving away this bewildering, confusing stranger and bringing back to life the strong, dynamic man she knew. His head went back proudly, the shadows clearing from his eyes so that they were cold and cutting, cruel as any knife.

'I love you, Grace. I always have, and I fear I always will. But that doesn't mean I'm going to act on it. I have never made decisions based on emotions and I certainly don't intend to start now!'

'That doesn't sound like any sort of love I've ever known!'

Love didn't talk of fear or refusing to act. Love just was; that was all.

'I don't believe you know what you're talking about.'

'*Christos*, Grace!' Constantine blazed, covering the ground between them with swift, angry strides. 'It is you who doesn't know what you are talking about!'

Reaching her side, he caught hold of her chin, lifting her face to his, studying it so intently that it seemed he wanted to commit every feature to memory in case he never saw it again.

'Loving you is not a choice I made. It's who I am. I could no sooner stop myself from loving you than I could will my heart to stop beating, my body to stop breathing. I think I fell in love with you in the first moment I saw you. In that moment I was lost and I knew I would never be the same again.'

Hearing that rawly voiced declaration of feeling, Grace felt as if her heart, every vital organ, even her breathing, had suddenly closed down, leaving her in a state of suspended animation. Her blood had frozen in her veins, holding her immobile. She couldn't think, could barely see his white drawn face, so close to her own. She could only focus on the fathomless pits that were his eyes, drawing her in deeper and deeper until she felt she was drowning in them.

Abruptly Constantine released his grip on her, his hand falling away to his side.

'But I do not intend to act on that emotion.'

At another time, in another existence, it seemed, she would have welcomed such an avowal of love, letting it fill her mind with an explosion of sheer delight. It should have made her heart soar, singing for joy, but the true effect it had was exactly the opposite.

What Constantine had given with one hand he had immediately snatched away with the other. No sooner had the words of love been spoken than he had revoked them, making them worse than worthless. And the pain was all the worse because just once she had heard him say what she'd most longed to hear. The words she had only ever heard him speak in her dreams over the past two and a half years.

'I don't believe you can do that!' It was a cry of anguish, all the bitter pain welling up inside and spilling out at last.

'Believe it!' he ordered coldly. 'I can do anything I want. That is where I do have a choice. I can decide what I'm going to do about the way I feel—whether I let it influence me.'

'Influence...?'

Grace lifted shaking hands to her head, pressing her fingers hard against her temples to ease the pain that throbbed there. It was as if someone had placed a steel band around her head and was tightening it slowly and inexorably, piling physical agony on top of the mental pain she felt.

'I—I don't understand.'

The breath hissed in through Constantine's clenched teeth in a sound of pure exasperation and he swung away from her, striding over to the bay window. He stared out into the dark, deserted street, much as he had done on the second morning after the party, the time when he had told her she would never be his wife. And just as it had done then, so now every taut line of his body screamed hostility and total rejection of her presence.

'I choose not to let myself feel this love,' he said at last, still keeping his face averted. 'I will not let it into my mind or my heart, or whatever other organ the purple-penned writers of poems or stories would have us believe harbours such an emotion.'

'How can you can do that?'

It was a sound of horror, of sheer incredulity, her wide, stunned eyes fixed on the tight muscles that hunched that normally long straight back.

Hearing it, Constantine moved suddenly, flexing his broad shoulders as if he felt the imprint of her gaze. Slowly he turned to face her, his features set into such a remote, expressionless mask that she didn't need an answer to her question. She could see it stamped into the white lines his ruthless control had etched around his nose and mouth.

'The way I feel is as much a fact of my life as that I am Greek, or that I have black hair, black eyes, and olive skin. It *is*. I can do nothing about it. But I have to get on with my life, so I refuse to let it even register on my thoughts. It is much the same as the fact that I am afraid of lifts, but I never give in to it.'

'You're...'

Momentarily diverted from her misery by this totally un-expected development, Grace could only stare at him in stunned bemusement. Had Constantine actually admitted to a failing, a weakness? She couldn't believe that he could ever be afraid of anything!

'You're afraid of…'

'Of lifts,' Constantine confirmed curtly with a swift, brusque movement of his head, as if challenging her to make something of it.

'But all the time I've known you—I'd never have guessed.'

'Precisely. I feel it, but I do not let it affect me.'

'And that's what you believe you can do with your feel-ings for me?'

'I do not feel—I know.'

'Oh, you know, do you?'

Just as it had on Skyros so much earlier that evening, once more anger proved her salvation. Feeling it run through her veins, warming, revitalising, driving away the fear and confusion that had held her frozen, she welcomed it gladly. Not giving herself time to think, she acted on its impetus, moving forward in a rush, heading straight for Constantine.

He watched her approach warily, his expression guarded, black eyes narrowed. But he didn't make any move, either towards her or away from her, and before she was quite ready she found herself close up against him; almost can-noning into the hard wall of his body before she actually managed to come to a halt.

'So you know that if I do this…'

Deliberately she lifted her hand and let it rest briefly on his shoulder before sliding it slowly and with deliberate sensuality down the length of his arm and on to his hand, gently smoothing over the warm skin, the strong muscles, the long bones. She felt his fingers move, just once, under her touch, then become still.

'Or this…'

Both hands moved to his face, caressing the lean planes of his cheeks, the tense jaw. Moving round to the nape of his neck, she wove her fingers into the dark silk of his hair, feeling its softness slide under her touch.

Silently Constantine watched her, ebony eyes hooded and withdrawn.

'Or even this…'

With her arms looped around his neck, she moved closer, pressing the softness of her body against the broad strength of his. Her breasts were crushed against his chest, her hips against his pelvis, and she could feel the heat and hardness of the immediate physical response he couldn't hide from her. It was there in the ragged nature of his breathing too, and the feverish slash of colour along the wide cheekbones.

'And, oh, Constantine…' she murmured in his ear. 'If I do this, then will you be able to control how you react?'

Her lips drifted from the corner of his jaw, over his cheekbone and down towards his mouth. But when she finally pressed the kiss she had been aiming for on to his lips, his response made her recoil in shocked dismay.

Or rather his lack of response. Because when she had been expecting the usual instantaneous response, the flaring passion, the searing demand, to feel his rock-hard stillness, the silent rejection of her caress, was like a blow in her face. She felt bruised and sullied, as if she had had her head slammed hard up against a granite cliff-face.

She couldn't move away quickly enough. She just couldn't bear to stay close to him, to touch him, feel the total rejection in every muscle, see it burning in those brilliant cyes.

'Point taken!' she flung at him, her voice raw with pain

as she put much needed distance between them. 'You certainly know how to get your message across.'

'Don't you English have a saying about being cruel to be kind?' Constantine returned with shocking imperturbability.

'Kind!' Grace spat the word out. 'There was nothing at all *kind* about what you just did.'

'I didn't want you to be under any illusions.'

'Oh, you needn't worry about that! I lost every trace of any illusions I had about you a long, long time ago.'

If only it was the truth. If only she really had had every foolish delusion stripped from her at the start. And she should have done. After all, Constantine had been totally straight with her. Brutally so, if she was honest with herself. It was only her foolish dream that things might be different that had got in the way.

'And that's why I think it would be better if we called a halt to this right here and now.'

It was obvious that he hadn't expected anything like that. His dark head went back sharply, black eyes narrowing in stunned disbelief.

'That isn't what I want.'

'Well, it's wha⸠ I want, damn you!'

Stubborn pride refused to let her show how much it hurt, giving her the courage to hold her head up high and look him straight in the face.

'Be honest, Constantine. It isn't working.'

'It seems to be working fine to me. This is exactly what our arrangement was supposed to be...'

'But it isn't *enough*!'

She even stamped her foot to emphasise the words. What did she have to do to get this through to him? If he continued to fight her, she didn't know how long she could hold out.

'What do you want? More money? Clothes? A better flat?'

Grace couldn't believe what she was hearing. Her head swam in horror so that she felt nauseous and weak. Did he really think that was all she needed?

'I don't want more *things*! I don't want jewels or clothes or to be set up in a luxury apartment like some long-ago courtesan kept by her lover!'

'Then what *do* you want? You only have to say.'

'I want…'

Tears blurred her vision, making it impossible to focus on his face, but she wouldn't let them fall, even though it meant she couldn't actually see his expression.

'I want what you can't give me,' she said despondently. 'I want a love that includes commitment and—and trust, and a hope of a future together. And we don't have that.'

'Grace…'

Constantine's swift strides took him across the room to her side. One hand closed around a slender wrist, the other clamping itself to her waist, holding her prisoner when she would have twisted away.

'Oh, Grace, what we do have is too good to lose.'

He was coming close. Too close. His warm lips were on her forehead, pressing heartbreakingly gentle kisses on her skin.

'Can you really bear to live without it?'

God help her, he had only to touch her and already she was melting. The dark enchantment that he wove so easily curled around every one of her senses, filling them with the sight, the sound, the scent of him.

Weakly she swayed into his arms, let him pull her close. The touch of his hands was like fire on her skin, burning through the fine material of her dress as his fingers circled her breast, teasing the already sensitive nipple into demanding life.

'You know how it can be. How it has been. How it can be again.'

'And marriage?' It was just a whisper, a thin thread of sound that he had to bend his proud head to hear.

'Marriage…'

He didn't need to answer. She could read his thoughts in his face, in the sudden closing up of those handsome features, the way heavy lids swiftly hooded his eyes.

'Grace, *agape mou…*'

The muttered endearment was the last straw. It slashed through the fog inside Grace's head, driving away the heated haze that had held her prisoner.

'No!'

With an effort that tore at her heart she wrenched herself out of his arms, driving herself halfway across the room as she did so. Unshed tears made her eyes brilliant as diamonds as she forced herself to face him, forced the words to her lips.

'No. It won't work! I can't do it! I can't live like that! I won't live like that. So it has to be over. I want it to be over. That way you can find someone you consider fit to be your wife and I—I…'

She couldn't finish the sentence. Couldn't claim that she too would find someone else. Because if she couldn't have Constantine, then there would be no one else she could ever love in the same way.

'Grace…'

Oh, why wouldn't he give in? Why wouldn't he go and leave her to break her heart in peace?

'No, Constantine,' she managed flatly, lifelessly, the words dragged up from the very bottom of her desolated soul. 'Don't say any more. There is nothing you can say. I've made up my mind and there's no way I'm going to change it. I want you to go.'

CHAPTER TWELVE

GRACE surveyed the scene before her with a faint grimace of distaste. The Henderson and Cartwright reception was in full swing, but she was really not in any mood for socialising. If she could have come up with a viable excuse for not attending, she would have seized on it gladly, but she knew that to miss what her employers considered the social event of the year was very definitely regarded as dereliction of duty. Like it or not, she was expected to turn up.

But her mood was very far from sociable. All she ever wanted to do these days was to get through her work as well as she could and then hurry home, lock the door, and leave the world behind.

Not that she could leave all of it behind. It didn't matter where she was or what she did, but the memory of Constantine and the way he had looked on the last day she had seen him came back to haunt her again and again. Even in her sleep he was there, tormenting her with a terrible sense of loss. Or, worse, she would dream of his lovemaking, enduring heated, erotic images that drove her nearly insane with pleasure and from which she would wake, shaking and sweating, in a tangle of bedclothes that were a mute testimony to the disturbed nature of her sleep.

But tonight she had done her duty, she told herself. It would be more honest to say that she had had enough. If she had to smile at one more client or pretend to listen to one more pompous managing director trying to tell her what was wrong with the country she would scream.

No one would see her go. They were all at the stage of the evening where the generous amounts of wine provided and a lavish buffet meant that no one was too clear about who was there and who wasn't. She could slip away quietly without being seen.

The air in the hotel garden was cool and fresh after the overheated smoky atmosphere inside. Grace drew in deep, appreciative breaths of it as she let the door swing to behind her, cutting off the sound of music and chatter in the ballroom she had just left. She would just take a couple of minutes' peace and quiet and then she would make her way to Reception and ask them to ring for a taxi to take her home.

'So this is where you've been hiding yourself!'

Oh, no, Grace groaned inwardly. Not again! Not now!

Les Harvey had been trying to flirt with her all evening. From the moment she'd arrived he had made a beeline for her, and had continued to dance attendance on her ever since. But, feeling as she did, she just wasn't in the right mood to handle him properly. And as one of the most important clients the agency had, Les Harvey had to be handled with kid gloves.

'I missed you in there. Looked round and you'd gone— like Cinderella, but no glass slipper.'

'I needed some fresh air.'

This was even worse than she'd imagined. Les had obviously been taking advantage of the free drinks provided, and he was decidedly more drunk than he had been when she had last seen him. His round face was flushed, his pale blue eyes glittered unnaturally, and the lank fair hair was plastered to his scalp by his own sweat.

'Oh, come now.' Les wagged a reproving finger so close to her face that she had to flinch back hastily in order to avoid it going into her eye. 'You've been teasing me all night, playing hard to get. I know a come-on when I see one.'

'A—a come-on! Mr Harvey,' Grace managed, praying

that the formality would put some necessary distance between them. Already he was invading her personal space with a vengeance, breathing heavily as he swayed on his feet, and peering down at the scooped neck of her black silk dress in a way that was an offence in itself. 'I was just going home.'

'Great idea.' Leaning forward suddenly, he planted a wet, slobbering kiss on her mouth. 'Your place or mine?'

Shocked and appalled, Grace took a hasty step backwards, out of reach.

'I think you've made a mistake...'

'No mistake.' One heavy hand clamped over her shoulder, the other capturing her chin and twisting it round so that she was forced to face him again. 'I know what you're after. I heard about you and Kiriashiz.'

'Constantine?' Even the sound of his name so mangled by this drunk was enough to weaken her, driving a wedge into the normally secure armour of composure she wore at work. 'What about—'

'Everyone knows you were his bit of stuff—that you sold yourself out to the highest bidder...' The hand on her shoulder began to move, pawing clumsily so that Grace shuddered in horror. 'But now he's dropped you—so naturally you're looking for someone else to be your sugar daddy.'

'No...'

Her protest went unheard. The hand that held her chin squeezed it hard, the thumb rubbing over and over her mouth, while the other hand slid down her back, exploring her hips, her buttocks. With an effort, Grace wrenched herself free.

'I said no!' she declared, all thought of trying to be polite driven from her mind. 'And I meant no. Take your hands off me, you filthy louse! I can't stand you touching me!'

She recognised her mistake, saw the danger it had put her in as soon as she saw his face change.

'What's this?' he snarled. 'Am I not good enough for you? Not rich enough, I should say. Well, let me tell you, darling, I may not have the Greek's millions, but I'm every bit the man he is, and I'll prove it…'

She saw what was coming but didn't dodge quite quickly enough. Moving with surprising speed, Les grabbed hold of her, pulling her roughly towards him.

Acting purely on instinct, Grace kicked out hard, a sense of triumph filling her as she heard his muffled grunt of pain. It was enough to distract him just long enough for her to wrench herself away. But she didn't get off scot-free. The large signet ring Les wore scraped uncomfortably over her skin, and a loud ripping sound told her that her freedom had been bought at the expense of the destruction of the top of her dress.

But she didn't care. All she could think about was getting away, putting as much distance between herself and Les Harvey as possible. Already he had recovered and she could hear his heavy footsteps behind her, his furious voice calling her every name under the sun. He was between her and the door back to the hotel, blocking her way there. Panic putting wings on her heels, she fled.

She had no idea how long she had been running for or how far she had come. She only knew that when the panic eventually subsided and her pace gradually slowed it was obvious that she had managed to leave her tormentor far behind. There was no sign of him along the whole length of the street, and now she was thinking again she vaguely remembered him tripping over something and falling face down on the ground.

But where was she? Where had her blind flight taken her? Had she escaped one peril only to plunge straight into another, even worse?

Looking round, she was stunned to find that she knew exactly where she was. She had been here many times in the past. The building ahead of her had once been where she had thought she would live at the start of her married life. It was the one where Constantine had his apartment.

Constantine. Just his name was an invocation, a charm, a form of protection against danger. She hadn't come here by accident. Like a small hunted animal, fleeing straight for its home, instinct had brought her here, to the only place where she could feel truly safe.

She didn't care any more about marriage or commitment. She only knew that she needed Constantine, that only he could fill the emptiness inside her. It was his arms that she needed round her, his strength that she wanted to lean against. If that was all he could give her, then she would welcome it and be happy with it. Because the truth was that she was dying without him.

'Oh, please let him be in!' she prayed as she pressed the bell that she knew would ring the security telephone in Constantine's apartment. 'Dear God, please, please let him be in!'

'Yes?' Curt, and clearly angry at being disturbed, Constantine's voice through the speaker was still the most wonderful, the most welcome sound she had ever heard.

'Constantine—it's Grace.'

Even from this distance she could sense the invisible Constantine's immediate withdrawal, his impulse to put the phone down on her.

'Please!' she said hurriedly. 'Please let me in! I—I need you.'

The silence that greeted her entreaty stretched out through perhaps a hundred fearful uneven heartbeats. Then, just as she was convinced that he would turn her away, reject her completely, she heard his sigh, a perfect blend of exasperation and resignation.

'Come up,' was all he said as he pressed the button to release the door-lock.

The journey up to the penthouse seemed endless, in spite of the speed of the fast, efficient lift. As she was carried upwards Grace suddenly remembered the last time she had seen Constantine, the way he had unwillingly admitted to his fear of being in this enclosed space.

So what on earth had possessed a man who hated lifts to buy an apartment at the very top of a high building? Had he done it simply to prove to himself that he could defy that fear, that, as he had declared so emphatically, he could refuse even to let it register on his mind while he got on with his life?

She still hadn't solved the problem when the lift came to a halt and she stumbled out into the brightly lit hallway of Constantine's apartment.

He was there, waiting for her, his clothes an un-Constantine-like white tee shirt and denim jeans, his face dark as a thundercloud.

'What the—?' he began ominously but then he took in her appearance fully and his expression changed abruptly.

'Grace!' This time his tone was very different. 'What the hell happened to you?'

His concern was the last straw. Suddenly all the tears she had managed to hold back until now were there. They coursed down her cheeks, unstoppable, blinding her so that all she could do was hold out her hands, groping for him desperately.

'Grace!'

Her hands were taken in a strong, warm grasp, and the next moment she was gathered into the comfort and safety of his arms. It was like a dream come true. *All* her dreams come true. And she couldn't tell if the convulsive sobs that broke from her were of remembered fear or pure joy at the sense of coming home at last.

She was scarcely aware of Constantine manoeuvring her into his flat, of him settling her on the settee and coming

down beside her. She only knew of his silent sympathy, his
support as he held her, gently stroking her hair, patiently
waiting for the storm of weeping to burn itself out.

When at last the racking sobs had subsided to intermit-
tent gasps and hiccups, and Grace found herself reduced to
sniffing inelegantly, he reached across for a box of tissues
and pulled out a handful, pushing some into her limp hand
and using another to wipe the tear stains from her cheeks.

'Do you feel ready to talk?' he asked softly. 'Can you
tell me what happened?'

His gentleness was almost more than she could bear. It
stole her tongue so that she could only shake her head in
despair, unable to say a word.

'*Christos*, Grace! You have to say something! You turn
up here—in this appalling state. You're shaking like a
leaf—and you won't say why! Oh God…!'

He caught himself up sharply, shaking his head in despair at his own foolishness.

'I'm sorry—that's the last thing you need. Forgive me,
sweetheart…'

But surprisingly his outburst had had the opposite effect
of the one he'd feared. Hearing the raw edge to his words,
something close to desperation in his tone, had jolted her
out of the frozen state of fear into which she had fallen.

When her tear-swollen eyes flickered open they looked
straight into his blazing black gaze, surprising there a look
of such uncertainty, such distress, that she was swamped
with an overwhelming need to help him rather than have
him help her. She felt she would do anything at all if only
to smooth that disquiet from his mind.

'It's—it's all right,' she managed shakily. 'Obviously
you need to…to…'

She had started out bravely enough, but now her voice
failed her again. With a muttered curse Constantine got to
his feet and moved to the far side of the room. Grace heard

the chink of a bottle against glass, and when he came back to her again it was to push a crystal brandy balloon into the limp fingers of her right hand.

'Drink that!' he commanded sharply.

'I don't like brandy!' It was a wail of protest.

'You don't have to like it, just drink the damn stuff!'

That was so much more like the Constantine she knew that it brought a weak smile to her quivering lips. This was her Constantine, the one she knew and loved.

'What did you say?'

To her consternation, Constantine's sharp ears had caught her foolish muttering of the words aloud.

'Nothing…'

She didn't feel strong enough to tell him yet. He might be anxious and concerned, but that was a natural enough reaction from anyone confronted by someone in the state she had been in when she'd arrived. She couldn't just blurt out the way she was feeling baldly and without any preparation.

So she forced herself to sip at the brandy, grimacing as the fiery liquid burned its way down her throat. It did make her feel better, she had to admit, feeling the warmth creep along her veins and drive away some of the bone-freezing cold she had been experiencing, for all that the night was so mild.

Constantine sat silently beside her, his long body held tensely so that she couldn't be unaware of the struggle he was having not to demand an explanation for her dramatic appearance at his home. But neither by word or gesture did he give any sign of impatience or attempt to push her into something she was not ready for, simply waiting until she turned to him again.

'I—I owe you an explanation—' she began, but broke off in shock as she saw him shake his head emphatically.

'You owe me nothing,' he said huskily. 'I was all sorts

of a fool even to ask. You came here obviously in distress,
too shocked to speak, and I come on like the counsel for
the prosecution, only making matters worse. Forgive me—
I was out of my mind with worry and I wasn't thinking
straight.'

'But I would like to tell you.' Her voice went up and
down in the most peculiar way in reaction to that *out of my
mind with worry*. 'I want you to know what happened.'

It didn't take very long. Strengthened by a few more
fortifying sips of brandy, she found that the whole sorry
tale tumbled out in a rush, with only a few stumbles here
and there over a particularly difficult bit.

She didn't even have to finish it. Because as soon as she
mentioned Les Harvey a dark, dangerous scowl descended
on to Constantine's beautifully carved features, and when
she touched on the assault on her he was there before her,
letting out a litany of rasping profanities, white-hot fury
blazing in his eyes.

'The bastard!' he roared, getting to his feet in a rush, his
anger too great to let him stay still. One clenched fist
slammed into the palm of the other hand with a violent
sound that made Grace wince inwardly.

'Constantine…' she began, but he simply ignored her.

'I will kill him,' he declared, his tone suddenly very different. The anger was still there, but now it was expressed
with a cold, deadly purpose that was somehow much more
frightening than the rage of seconds earlier. 'I will push his
filthy words down his throat and I'll—'

'Constantine, no! You mustn't! That isn't what I want!'

At first she thought that he hadn't heard her again, but
then, slowly, he turned to her, obviously reining in his
fierce temper only with considerable effort.

'The police, then.' It was a statement, not a question.

'No. Not that either. I—I don't want you to do anything.'

'Not do anything! But, Grace, look at yourself! How can I let a man do that to you and not want to punish him?'

His wild gesture towards her with his hand made Grace look down at herself for the first time since reaching the sanctuary of Constantine's apartment. Her breath stilled, her eyes widening as she saw just what Constantine meant.

The neck of the black dress was torn wide open, a large flap of material hanging loose so that the lace of her bra was exposed. And where the signet ring had caught her, the white flesh was raised in an ugly red weal.

'It looks worse than it is—it does!' she insisted when he looked frankly sceptical, his expression refuting the truth of her declaration. 'I was frightened, shocked, but he didn't really hurt me. Please, Constantine, leave it! I just want to forget that tonight ever happened.'

He was strongly tempted to ignore her appeal. Rejection flared in his eyes, fought a fierce battle with reason, and finally, she was thankful to see, conceded defeat.

'If that is what you want,' he said reluctantly. 'But if anyone other than you had asked me...'

The way his right hand closed again into a tight, clenched fist revealed the violence of his feelings more eloquently than any words, and Grace couldn't suppress a shiver of reaction at the thought of that icy fury turned on anyone—even Les Harvey.

'It's what I want, Constantine,' she confirmed shakily. 'Really, it is. If you love me—'

Oh, no! How had that slipped out? Panic flared in her mind as she wished the foolish words back, but it was too late.

'If I love you!' Constantine echoed on an odd note, one she couldn't begin to interpret. 'Grace, I have told you how I feel.'

Love, but no commitment. The sort of love he would bend ruthlessly to his will, as he had his fear of lifts. Well, she'd already told herself tonight that she would accept that. It was that or nothing. And she couldn't live with nothing.

'I...' she began, but suddenly he was shaking his head.

'I cannot give you any more than I have already.'

'I understand,' Grace whispered, struggling to make her voice audible.

'I wonder if you do,' he responded enigmatically.

Suddenly he moved, coming to sit beside her again, taking both of her hands in his and closing his fingers over them.

'Grace, will you answer one question?'

'If I can. What do you want to know?'

'Just this—why are you here tonight?'

'Why?' Grace frowned her confusion. 'You know why! Because Les—'

'But why did you come *here*? Why not go to your friends or to Ivan?'

'I couldn't go anywhere else,' she said simply and honestly. 'As soon as I started thinking again, I knew I wanted to be with you and only you. And I knew you'd be there for me. Constantine—what is it?'

He had dropped his face into his hands, bronzed fingers hiding his eyes from her.

'Theos!' he groaned in harsh self-reproach. 'I have been so blind!'

'Blind? Constantine, please, I don't understand!'

Slowly he straightened his head, and when he took his hands away there was something new in his eyes. Or, rather, not new, but the expression she had once seen there every day, in the days leading up to their wedding. The days before Paula.

Then she would have called it love; now she did not dare to put so emotive a name on it.

'Trust,' was all he said, his accent strangely thick, his voice cracking on the single word.

'Trust?' Grace echoed shakily, her mind whirling, but Constantine pressed a gentle hand over her mouth to silence her when she would have said more.

'Please, just listen,' he begged. 'I have so much to tell you. So much you need to know. Please listen and then answer me one question.'

Even when he took his hand away again Grace couldn't find the words to answer him, but simply nodded silently, tension making her heart beat high up in her throat. She couldn't be in any doubt that what he was about to say was terribly important. It was written all over Constantine's taut face, etched into it by the strain that pulled his beautiful skin tight over those amazing cheekbones.

'I think perhaps I'd better start with my grandfather.'

'Your grandfather?' She'd resolved to stay silent, but this was such a surprise that she couldn't stop herself from reacting. 'What has he got to do with this?'

'More than you could imagine. You remember I told you how he was such an influence on me when I was growing up? Well, one of the things that he instilled into me was the fact that I should never sit back and rest on my laurels—or, rather, his laurels. That just because the Kiriazis family was now so wealthy, we should never take our fortune for granted. We had been poor once; we could be so again. He always quoted the old saying: rags to riches and back again in three generations.'

'He needn't have worried about that with you.' Grace's voice was shaky. She didn't quite see where this was leading. 'After all, if your grandfather made a fortune, you've made a second one all of your own.'

'Yes, but that was only half of what he taught me.'

Constantine pushed a hand through his hair, ebony eyes

slightly unfocused, as if they were looking back into the past.

'The other thing he wanted for me was a marriage like his. He met my grandmother when he was nineteen, and they were together for over sixty years. She married him when he was just a woodcarver, but she died the wife of a very rich man...'

Long fingers fretted at the strap of the gold watch on his wrist, betraying a lack of composure that was otherwise hidden by his rigid self-control.

'When he gave me this watch, he made me swear to him that I would never marry unless I was absolutely sure. That only when I met someone who I believed had as much faith in me as my grandmother had had in him would I make her my wife. I gave him my word.'

'Oh!'

It was a long sigh of comprehension and distress. Now she saw exactly what had motivated Constantine. How he had felt bound by the promise he had made to his grandfather, and how her own actions had led him to believe that she was not the sort of woman the old man had wanted for him.

'I understand,' she said softly. 'I see now why you can't offer me marriage, but it no longer matters—'

'Of course it matters!' Constantine broke in on her harshly. 'It matters like hell! Because I have been so wrong, so stupid, so out of my head blind not to see what was right before my eyes. I wanted to kill that rat Harvey, but the truth is that I have behaved every bit as badly as he has. When you told me about tonight, it was like looking in a mirror, and, believe me, I didn't like what I saw. There are some pretty ugly similarities between my behaviour and the pig who—'

'No!' Grace couldn't let him continue, and this time it was she who laid a finger on his lips. 'Constantine, no!'

'Yes!'

With an angry gesture he twisted away from her restrain-
ing hand, grabbing at it and holding it and its partner tightly
in his lap.

'All I offered you was money and sex. I claimed to love
you, but I let my pride blind me to the truth. Right from
the start, I believed that if you loved me you would never
doubt me, not even for a second, and yet I doubted you,
but I was too damn proud to admit it. That day you came
to confront me, after Paula spewed out all her filthy lies, I
didn't try hard enough to convince you. Instead, I saw the
whole thing as a test of your love. A test I had no right at
all to set.'

'But I failed...'

'No.' Constantine shook his dark head violently. 'No, I
failed you. Because deep down I was afraid. I was terrified
that you might not love me as much as I believed. That
you might actually believe I was capable of being so faith-
less, so heartless...'

'If that was fear then you hid it very well.'

Just as he had always hidden the way he felt about being
in a lift, refusing to let it show, believing that if he refused
to acknowledge its existence it wouldn't affect his life.

'You just looked cold, and so very distant.'

'That was just a mask,' Constantine assured her. 'And
behind it was the fear—total, gut-wrenching panic—that
and a terrible sense of guilt.'

'Guilt?' Grace echoed, looking back, seeing him again
on that dreadful day, seeing that momentary flash of something in his eyes, the look that she had believed betrayed
his lack of innocence at the time.

'I felt guilty at treating you that way. Somewhere deep
inside I was ashamed of the way I was behaving, and the
fact that I was hurting you so much, but I would rather

have died than admit it. I let my pride get in the way of everything and so I lost you.'

Black eyes locked with grey, holding her mesmerised with the intensity of feeling that burned there. She couldn't speak, could hardly breathe. Even her heart seemed to have stopped beating, so fiercely was she concentrating on what he was saying.

'I went away, told myself I could forget you. But I couldn't get you out of my mind. After two years I just couldn't take it any longer. Any one of a dozen people could have sorted out the problems in the London office, but I snatched at the chance to come back to England, and Ivan's invitation to the party gave me the perfect opening I was looking for. But I would have found you anyway. I couldn't live without you.'

Releasing one of her hands, he reached out to touch her cheek, his caress infinitely gentle.

'And still my damn stupid pride got in the way. That was why I forced you into that appalling arrangement. I would have done anything I could to keep you with me for as long as possible.'

His thumb smoothed over her skin, erasing the last traces of the storm of tears, his expression watchful and concerned,

'I told myself I wanted proof that you truly loved and trusted me, when all the time it was right there before my eyes in the fact that you took me back, the way you behaved, the way you let me treat you. But I couldn't see it. I couldn't even see my own feelings clearly. But I knew my mother would. That was why I rushed you away from Skyros. I knew that if she took one look at my face she would see that I was still crazy about you—and there was no way she'd keep quiet about it. And then tonight...'

The words deserted him as he shook his head in despair at his own behaviour. But Grace didn't need an explanation.

Now she saw just what that single word 'trust' meant. Her instinctive, unthinking flight into Constantine's protection had provided the proof of the faith in him he had needed so much.

'Grace, my love, forgive me. Forgive my blind stupidity, my arrogant pride, my ignorance, my—'

She couldn't let him continue with the litany of self-reproach, but stopped his mouth with her own, making it clear that no words were necessary, that he hadn't needed to ask.

'And you must forgive me my doubts,' she whispered against his lips. 'I should have known that the man I love could never have done those appalling things. And I do love you, Constantine. I love you so much it hurts even to think about it.'

They were the last words she said for some time. Because even before she had spoken the last one Constantine had taken her mouth again in a hot, yearning kiss. A kiss that led to a thousand other kisses, each of them more passionate than the first. And those kisses led to caresses, the caresses to openly urgent demand.

Without quite knowing how it had happened, Grace found herself on Constantine's bed, her clothes discarded somewhere she neither knew nor cared. All she felt was that this was where she truly belonged, that this was her heart's one real home, the place she had been born to find, the destiny that had always awaited her.

And as she welcomed the fierce, primitive thrust of Constantine's body into hers she could not hold back a cry of sheer delight and wonder at the thought that this was the first time they had truly made love together. That for the first time their minds and hearts were united as well as their physical selves.

'One thing puzzles me,' she murmured a long time later

when, their hunger sated, they were lying, heavy-limbed with exhaustion, in each other's arms.

'And what is that, *agape mou*?' Constantine's voice was thick with satisfaction, lazy as his strong body, lying tangled up with her own.

'You said you had a question you wanted me to answer. What was that?'

'Couldn't you guess?' he teased softly. 'Isn't there only one possible question it could be? I wanted to know if you would marry me. If you would do me the very real honour of becoming my wife.'

'Your wife!' The shock brought her upright in the bed to look down into his dark face in stunned confusion. 'But you said that you couldn't give me that...'

'I said I couldn't give you any more than I have already,' Constantine corrected gently. 'Because it would be impossible. How can I give you any more when you already have it all? When my heart, my mind, my body, even my very soul are totally enslaved by you? I would give you the world if I could...'

'I told you, I don't need *things*,' Grace reminded him, her heart singing in unbounded joy. 'If you want to give me anything, a wedding ring will be more than enough. That, and perhaps the twelve autumn leaves you promised me for every year of our married life. No?' she asked in confusion as Constantine shook his head against the pillow, his mouth curving into a warm smile.

'Don't you know you have them already as well? The necklace I gave you—the leaves are real. I collected them for you before we broke up and had them preserved in gold so that they would last for ever. They were to have been my present to you on the day we married.'

'I'll wear them on my wedding day,' Grace promised, bending her head to kiss him again.

They would have no need of such superstitions in the future, she knew. Once she was Constantine's wife, every day of every year to come was guaranteed to be happy ever after.

If you enjoyed what you just read,
then we've got an offer you can't resist!

Take 2 bestselling love stories FREE!

Plus get a FREE surprise gift!

Come escape with Harlequin's new
Series Sampler

Four great full-length Harlequin novels bound together in one fabulous volume and at an unbelievable price.

Be transported back in time with a Harlequin Historical® novel, get caught up in a mystery with Intrigue®, be tempted by a hot, sizzling romance with Harlequin Temptation®, or just enjoy a down-home all-American read with American Romance®.

You won't be able to put this collection down!

On sale February 2000 at your favorite retail outlet.

HARLEQUIN®
Makes any time special ™

Visit us at www.romance.net

PHESC

Coming in January 2000
Classics for two of your favorite series.

SECRET
VOWS by REBECCA YORK
&
KELSEY ROBERTS

From the best of Rebecca York's

43
Light St.

Till Death Us Do Part

Marissa Devereaux discovered that paradise wasn't all it was cracked up to be when she was abducted by extremists on the Caribbean island of Costa Verde.... But things only got worse when Jed Prentiss showed up, claiming to be her fiancé.

From the best of Kelsey Roberts's

THE
ROSE
TATTOO

Unlawfully Wedded

J.D. was used to getting what he wanted from people, and he swore he'd use that skill to hunt down Tory's father's killer. But J.D. wanted much more than gratitude from his sassy blond bride—and he wasn't going to clue her in. She'd find out soon enough...if she survived to hear about it.

Available January 2000 at your favorite retail outlet.

HARLEQUIN®
Makes any time special ™

London's streets aren't just paved with gold—they're home to three of the world's most eligible bachelors!

You can meet these gorgeous men, and the women who steal their hearts, in:

NOTTING HILL GROOMS

Look out for these tantalizing romances set in London's exclusive Notting Hill, written by highly acclaimed authors who, between them, have sold more than 35 million books worldwide!

Irresistible Temptation by Sara Craven
Harlequin Presents® #2077
On sale December 1999

Reform of the Playboy by Mary Lyons
Harlequin Presents® #2083
On sale January 2000

The Millionaire Affair by Sophie Weston
Harlequin Presents® #2089
On sale February 2000

Available wherever Harlequin books are sold.

HARLEQUIN®
Makes any time special ™

GREEK TYCOONS

Wealth, power, charm—what else could a handsome tycoon need? Over the next few months, each of these gorgeous billionaires will meet his match... and decide that he has to have her— whatever it takes!

Meet Constantine, Dio, Andreas and Nikolas in:

On sale January 2000: **Constantine's Revenge**
by KATE WALKER
Harlequin Presents, #2082

On sale March 2000: **Expectant Bride**
by LYNNE GRAHAM
Harlequin Presents, #2091

On sale May 2000: **The Tycoon's Bride**
by MICHELLE REID
Harlequin Presents, #2105

On sale June 2000: **The Millionaire's Virgin**
by ANNE MATHER
Harlequin Presents, #2109

Available at your favorite retail outlet.

HARLEQUIN®
Makes any time special™